Genny in a Bottle

what to do when your best friend hates you

D1113452

Genny in a Bottle

what to do when your best friend hates you

Kristen Kemp

an apple paperback

SCHOLASTIC INC.

New York Toronto London Auckland Sydney
Mexico City New Delhi Hong Kong

To MeMe, a spunky gal who has
genie'd so many

ISBN 0-439-21179-4

12 11 10 9 8 7 6 5 4 3 2 1   0 1 2 3 4 5/0

Printed in the U.S.A.
First Scholastic printing, November 2000

Chapter 1
"It's Me Again!"
by Genny the Genie

I am so glad that I am alive. I mean, how many people get to say they've been on the earth for more than a thousand years? Even after all of that time, I can say, Yes, I do like it here.

Maybe that's because I recently met a girl named Nadia. Hanging with people like her makes me happy. And she totally renewed my faith in the genie business. After one thousand years — that's how long I've been doing this job, no lie — I was *so* ready to throw in my ponytail and call it quits. I'd had it up to my lip gloss with all of the things that kids want. I was also worn out from constantly adapting to the world's changes. I mean, do you know how long it took me to learn to program a VCR?! And don't even get me started on microwaves — those things freak me out.

But I don't feel fed up anymore. I really don't. After taking a few months off without a calling

1

— that's the feeling I get when someone needs me — I met my friend Nadia. Since I left her a while ago, I've been itching to get out of this bottle and do it all over again. I mean, I can only watch MTV in ten different languages so many times. And soaps! Why do they always use the same old story lines? Sheesh — you'd think the world's screenwriters could be more creative. I don't even feel like working on my dad's old wizard spells from the year 1000. I just feel like busting this joint and doing my job. I am ready to rescue a distressed damsel from a fire-breathing dragon. Or take a kid on an expedition to discover a new continent. Maybe I could help a young princess win back her kingdom from her creepy boyfriend king-wanna-be. But, hey . . . beggars can't be choosers. Those kinds of assignments just don't exist anymore. So I'd also be happy just to help a chick find her place in this world or give a boy some pointers on painful family problems. The stuff I've done in the last century isn't always as dramatic as those Old World assignments. But hey, to today's kids, their dilemmas are every bit as important.

Whoa! All of that thinking was tiring me out. Heavy-duty philosophizing was wearing down the batteries in my brain. So maybe I didn't want to go back to work right away. I figured

I'd just lie around for a while in my bottle (named Throttle). I can't say I *minded* curling up with my snippy kitty, Catfish, and taking weeklong naps. Rest and rejuvenation is a genie's right, right? Besides, I had to wait for a calling. I'd just relax until one came.

Or maybe I wouldn't. I thought I was experiencing an earthquake. Things began to violently tremble. Catfish dug his claws deep into my thigh to keep from falling off my lap. Ouch! I was freaked at first because earthquakes and other natural disasters don't typically strike genies in our bottles. Then it occurred to me that nothing was natural about what was happening. There were a series of *thump-thumps* on the walls. The vibrations made my teeth numb. It sounded like the pitter-patter of someone's fingers.

"Wait one minute!" I yelled impatiently. "Is someone shaking my bottle?"

That was not how it was supposed to work. *I* always get a calling, then *I* follow it. I am not supposed to be shaken and surprised by humans. I get to choose them, they *don't* get to choose me!

"Throttle, what in a fiddler's name is going on here?" I screamed again so rudely.

"What do you mean you don't know?" I asked after Throttle had responded. "I am requesting a new bottle tomorrow, I swear. I need one that's halfway modern."

"What? You want me to shut my trap? *S'il vous plaît!* I oughtta . . ."

In my rush of complaining, I knew there was no stopping what was about to happen. I was being discovered whether I liked it or not. Now, this was highly unusual. In all my years, I'd only been uncovered without my knowledge or permission once — and that was because Throttle had a bad crack he was busy repairing. Usually, we stay incognito until the time is right.

I mean, I wanted to go back to work, but not right that minute! My hair was a mess! I wanted to lie on my lazy genie bed for another few days. I NEEDED A NAP!

Oh my goodness! Oh my *goodness!* Ugh. *Ugh! UGH!*

The rattling got worse. I got more and more annoyed and frantic-feeling.

I screamed so loudly my throat went raw. "Just rub the darn thing and get it over with!"

Chapter 2
"Introducing . . . Us!"
by the *Best* Best Friends

Summers are made for best friends, there's no doubt about it. It's about having nonstop fun and laughing until our eyes and bellies absolutely ache. It's all about being free from everyone and everything — nobody bothers us, and we don't have to study for silly tests that just stress us out.

The best part is, school doesn't have to cross our minds for one second — and that's good because books usually, like, bore us. Instead, we're very busy from day to day with all of the ultra-important things we have to do. We like to write stories, make scrapbooks, do our nails, try on clothes, and watch TV. Oh, we like to dance and sing, too. Like, last week, we spent so many days learning all of the moves to the new Madonna video that we finally got it down, like, almost better than the star herself. We like to go down to the beach and try out our dances

— the spot we go to is private and only the ocean can see.

We are so busy that we don't really have time to make other friends. We do *everything* together — the two of us. And it takes every waking moment of the day to keep up! Besides, having more buds just means everything is messy. Like, one friend wants to go here, another wants to go there — then the third doesn't want to go anywhere. Who needs it?

Oops, we just realized that we're rude. We didn't even tell you our names. We're Molly and Marina. We live in a really lame, *bor*-ing little town in Maine. Everything here is quiet and calm — and freezing cold — until summertime comes. Then our tired town gets crowded and sucks even more because it's taken over by tourists. We don't like that one bit. But there's not much we can do about it since Molly's family rents out vacation houses, and Marina's family has a restaurant. It's not like you can move when you're thirteen years old. We keep asking to get our own place but our moms won't let us. They think we're kidding. Um, hello! We're not! What makes things worse is that our parents always tell us to be thankful for the stinky tourists. Can't you see how thankful we are!? Ha! At least our parents are very busy in the summer, which means we get more freedom than a lot of teens. Now *that's* something we don't complain about. Marina's parents also gave us this old shed outside the restaurant that's right on our private beach. We totally re-decorated it — and now it's the only place we ever go. We call it our beach clubhouse.

Okay, so let's get to the point of why you need to know us. When the day started out, we were determined to get to work on our art project. Well, Molly wanted to work on her I Love Lance scrapbook — she thinks of nothing other than him half the time, and the other half of the time she's watching reruns of his TV show. But after a long, hard discussion, we decided that doing a kickin' job on the art doohicky was more important. See, our parents say we waste all of our time together — even though they know absolutely nothing about all of the meaningful things we do. But anyway, they made us — literally screaming and crying — enroll in this teen art workshop at a local college. It's, like, three days a week all summer. All of the kids from school — the ones we try so desperately to avoid — are there, too. We were not one bit pleased about this at the time. To be completely honest, though, we secretly love our workshop. We've made really cool collages for our rooms and we created colorful abstract works of modern art. Best of all, though, was learning how to create the coolest earrings and necklaces out of beads and wires. Now we have to do a final project — and we want ours to be the best. The problem is, these lowlife girls in our class named Kristy and Keri want their project to be the best, too.

They're best friends like we are — but that's where the similarities end. To be compared to them would make us more sick than studying does. They have been competing with us since we were all in kindergarten. We're above it all, of course, but Kristy and Keri are always trying to strut their stuff in front of us. We swear, we really hate them. Like yesterday, they knew how much we love making necklaces — everybody knows it. And these two are just not fashionable like we are, no matter how hard they try. Anyway, they copied off us and started making jewelry that looked *just like ours*. We were so disgusted that we had to go home to lie down and hyperventilate.

So, see, don't you agree? Who *would* like wanna-bes like them? We really can't take those two girls, even though everyone tells us that disliking people is wrong. What does everyone else know? They don't have Kristy and Keri trying to outdo their every move! They even try to talk to our one friend, Justin, all of the time. He's Molly's cousin, so we pretty much have to be nice to him. He comes over from time to time. I guess we like him — but it's not fun doing makeovers when he's around.

So anyway, we needed to think hard about this final art project — it had to be genius. Like, even more creative than the too-cute, prizewinning robot that Justin made out of aluminum foil last school year. We decided to spend the morning really concentrating on this. Yes, Molly voluntarily put away her scrapbook. To put us in the mood for deep thought, we *feng shui*'d Marina's room with fresh wildflowers and a minty-scented candle. Then we made our minds focus and focus and focus.

Nothing came to us. The space between our ears was totally, completely blank. We turned to cable for inspiration. After about an hour of watching cartoons — please don't tell anyone that we still watch them — we put on our suits, packed our sandwiches, and headed out for a day at the beach. We were really hoping that the sun could give us some good ideas, since the wildflowers sure didn't work. There's a lot of vitamin D in sunlight, right? We decided that vitamins could definitely help us think better. And maybe we were right — we ended up being super-glad we went to the beach.

You see, when we got there, we found the strangest, coolest thing!

Chapter 3
"Here I Go Again – Times Two!"
by Genny the Genie

While my bottle was being so rudely rubbed, I heard the sounds and squeals of two girls goofing around. They were laughing and saying the word *like* a lot. I was busy yelling at Throttle. He needed to work his magic and make us disappear or something. My brain and whole body hadn't stopped rattling, which gave me a headache. I wanted it all to go away. Catfish was not helping matters. He hissed and snarled like a spoiled brat cat. He even chomped down on Throttle — a big no-no. So Throttle refused to do anything and said we deserved what we were about to get. Hmph. What a mess!

It was *not* turning out to be a relaxing day.

Then, *poof*! You know what happened next.

10

Three rubs and I was ejected from my very own bottle.

I was so embarrassed. My hair was a rodent's nest, and I had a white spot on my cheek where I was letting zit cream soak into my skin. I was even wearing my ratty old chicken pajamas. And without any warning, there I was, standing in front of two really cute girls on what appeared to be a deserted beach.

One girl, the one with dark skin and curly black hair, was jumping up and down. She was gasping for breath. The other one, a pretty little quiet-looking thing, stood there with her jaw open. Then the curly-headed one fell down on the ground.

"Oh my God, Marina! Are you okay?" the quiet one yelled, not so quiet anymore. "Do you need mouth-to-mouth or something?"

"Ewww! No!" she screamed. "I'm okay, Molly. I just tripped."

"Oh good. I'm glad that's all."

Then they both jumped up and down and squeaked sharply. They held on to each other's shoulders as they did it. No doubt, this was getting ancient fast.

"Yoo-hoo! I'm a genie, and I'm over here," I said.

"Oh, yeah, you," the curly-headed one said as

she gasped for breath again. "What are you? Who are you? Is this real or did we, like, eat some bad Pixie Sticks?"

"As I said, I am a genie, and I live in that bottle you just picked up. By the way, that bottle is not yours, and maybe you both should have kept your hands off of it." I didn't mean to sound so grouchy — but that's exactly how I felt. I was getting moodier by the nanosecond.

"Did you hear that, Molly!?" the curly-headed one asked.

"Yes, I did, Marina," the less outgoing one (must've been Molly) replied.

"We have a genie!"

"You mean just like that blond chick on the TV show? Can she, like, wiggle her nose and do anything she wants to do?"

"No, Molly, that's the other show about the witch."

"Oh, brother," I muttered. That old program sets genies back at least two thousand years. I know genies haven't had to marry their masters in my time!

"I get it! So she's like the one in *Aladdin*. OhmyGod! OhmyGod! She can make all of our wishes come true!" Molly yelled.

"You got it, girlfriend," Marina retorted, giving her friend a gleeful high five as if she'd just won something.

Grrr . . . I was losing my composure. They didn't even say hello to me! I stood there, being completely ignored, while they chanted, "We've got a genie. We've got a genie."

"First of all," I said, interrupting them. They continued to ignore me. So I sent Catfish to nip at their ankles. They screamed. "Do I have your attention now?" I asked.

"Oh, yes, yes. You have our attention," the one named Molly said.

"Wait one second," Marina cut in. "Do we have *your* attention? You're *our* genie, after all."

My, my. This was not going to be easy. I decided to approach this situation with the utmost dignity. "Listen here, girl-*amie*," I said. "First of all, I am only indebted to one of you."

"No, you're not," Marina said. "We both rubbed your bottle at the same time. You have to obey us."

I looked at them and tried to feel the genie Force. I couldn't figure out which girl was pulling me. I thought hard — I can always tell who is my kid customer. Then, to my horror, I knew it was both of them. I felt it — Marina was right. I can only think of one other time in all of my long history that I've had two masters. If I remember correctly, it was not a fun assignment. See, I had a calling from these two sisters in Ireland. It seemed like an easy enough

assignment — the usual missing-parent situation. So we took a little sea voyage . . . on the
Titanic! If that wasn't bad enough, they were on
opposite sides of the ship when it hit the 'berg.
Needless to say, it took more than my usual
brawn and muscle to find them both and get
them to the appropriate lifeboats. I swear, there
were moments when I thought my heart would
not go on. I thought back on that disaster
with the utmost panic. Not only was it one of
my most completely exhausting assignments, it
was also against every genie rule in the book.

"Oh my goodness, oh my goodness," I said.
This time, *I* was freaking out. This was going to
be embarrassing when the whole genie world
heard about this. They'd all say stuff like, "Look
at Genny, she's in double-trouble again!" Sure,
genies may seem sweet to outsiders, but that's
because we save our mean streaks for other
genies.

"Are we right?" Molly asked. "Are we both
your masters?"

I didn't say anything, just nodded.

"We get three wishes, Molly! *Three!*"

They started popping off about all of the
things they wanted. Molly yelled that she would
die to have some famous sitcom boyfriend and
that she'd be very pleased if I could give her
good, strong fingernails. Marina yelled that she

needed a new killer haircut and asked if I could do it quickly. I think I heard Molly ask Marina if they should be sweet girls and ask me to destroy all nuclear weapons for the good of the world. Then Marina assured her not to worry — someone's Website would surely try to stop the earth's destruction. They happily changed the subject and talked about finally getting their own place together, complete with an electronic closet and a winterized Jacuzzi. They also wanted their own private stylist.

"Oh, brother," I muttered. Okay, so they weren't brain surgeons. Fine. But I couldn't deal with them not getting the point of having me. I was there to improve and happify their lives — not make ten zillion superficial (read: supershallow) changes. Did they even know that deeper meanings in life existed? Was anything beyond nail polish important? I just wasn't so sure. . . .

Chapter 4
"Our Genie Isn't So Rude After All."
by Molly and Marina

We couldn't figure it out. Why wasn't our new genie as excited as we were? But we couldn't be bothered with our genie's mood, so we just walked toward our private clubhouse on the beach, and we commanded her to follow us.

This was going to be so much fun! No same-old, same-old summer for us! We were going to do everything we always wanted to do. On the way to the beach clubhouse, we envisioned yachts, our own lighthouse, and a limo with our very own driver. We thought we'd wish to be movie stars or models or even astronauts. We were nearly crying because we were so over-whelmed by the endless possibilities. We cry a lot but this time it was totally for real.

But it was getting more and more disappointing the longer that our genie went without speaking to us. We decided that maybe we needed to be more gentle with her. After all, she had just come out of the ocean, and it was only, like, thirty degrees in there! Didn't anyone tell her that you can't really go for a good swim in Maine unless you're in a heated pool?

We started asking her questions — real sweet ones.

"Would you like some lemonade?" Molly asked. "How about some pizza?" Pizza is our favorite food, and we were getting hungry. We hoped she'd be getting the munchies soon, too. At least her eyes lit up, and she didn't look so sad when we mentioned foodies.

"I would like some pizza with pepperoni, please," the beaten-down genie said. "And please get a few extra slices for my cat."

Okay, she *was* weird. But we did it anyway. We locked her in our clubhouse and went out to grab a bite. We couldn't help but notice how unglam she was. She had on pink pajamas with chickens on them! We raced back because we started getting more and more curious about this situation. To our surprise, our genie had transformed herself and now looked gorgeous. She had brushed her hair and changed into too-cute embroidered jeans with rainbows on the back pockets and a bright pink tank. Her

17

thick, shiny hair was high on her head in a ponytail. Her clothes were just killer. She was very skilled in the style department — she could teach teen mags a thing or two! She definitely looked like a new, improved genie since we left her, only, like, five minutes before.

"Sit down," she said in a tone that made us mad, but we didn't dare disobey. "I've got a few things to tell you."

"Okay, we have, like, fifty million questions!" we said, trying to be sweet.

"Ask them later," she answered. Ouch! "You didn't even ask me my name. It's Genny!"

We'd hurt her feelings! "We're sorry! We really should have done that."

Sometimes we just get too excited and forget our manners — we really need to work on that.

"Okay, I'm going to tell it to you like it is," Genny went on. "I'm a genie, as you know. And I am not in any way accustomed to having two masters. So I may not know exactly what I'm doing. But I will tell you that I am, indeed, yours." She took a long sigh, brushed loose hairs off her face, and said, "I think we got off to a wrong start. So let's start over again. *S'il vous plaît?*"

"Wow! Was that Spanish? That's so cool," I said.

"No, honey, it's French."

"Does that mean you know how to give French manicures?"

"I am a genie, not a beautician. Painting nails is not my job, but I'll do it under certain circumstances. As far as beauty goes, as you will find out, I have amazing taste in clothes. But don't think I perform just any old duty. I'll only do things when I'm asked appropriately and when the things are not mean in any way, shape, or form.

"I am not a miracle worker, either. I cannot just wiggle my hips and make you millionaires or give you great boyfriends. I can't do any of that."

"Oh, no! That's such a bummer!" we yelled, disappointed.

"You can't set me up on, like, just one date with Lance from my favorite show?"

"No, I'm sorry, unless you already know him, I can't. But wait . . . I can help make things come true that maybe wouldn't be possible without me."

"Like what?" we asked.

"That's your job. You tell me."

Once again, we thought and thought and thought. This was going to take a long time. Maybe this genie stuff wasn't so great. No mansion? No movie stars? Hmph. But we did think this Genny chick was pretty cool. And we never think that *anyone* is cool.

She forked over a handbook — and it told us all about the rules of having a genie. We found out that only we can see her, unless we choose to let one or two of our friends in on our secret. Like, no way! If we had other friends, do you think we'd tell them our secrets? What would be the point when we have each other? Also, we were so relieved to hear that our parents wouldn't find out about Genny — she said they couldn't see or hear her. Bonus! We were majorly impressed when we heard that she is the Year 1000 Genie and that only thirteen-year-olds like us have the ability to rub her bottle named Throttle and get her out. As far as rules go, we found out that we couldn't ask her to dance around naked — as if we'd really do that! — or ask her to do our laundry. Shucks! We'd get her for twenty-eight days, then she had to leave. But if she finished up earlier she'd have to go ahead of schedule. All of the details made our minds mushy! Another rule: We couldn't ask her to do mean things, either. That was okay, because we are not usually mean types of girls. We know we are self-absorbed and we could probably be a little nicer, but we're not mean. She let us know that pizza was expected at all times — and she liked pepperoni on it. That was fine. We practically eat pizza every day anyway.

"But what does that cat need Q-Tips for?" we asked.

"I can never tell you that," Genny said.

We really had no clue what we were getting ourselves into. But at least it wasn't lame-o boring stuff! Okay, so it would definitely take a major adjustment for us to have someone else around. But she was a genie, so we figured it would be okay. After all, genies are meant to make things go super-smoothly.

Or at least that's what we thought!

Chapter 5
"What Don't They Want?"

by Genny the Genie

We ate pizza — and things started going a little smoother. It was too early to tell if I'd make good friends with these two. They were very different from me. They didn't like poetry — or even know who Christina Rossetti was. I figured I could live with that because at least they liked to get down and dance. They even had a radio and CD player in their beach clubhouse. It was small, but I dug it. The walls were painted bright pink, blue, and yellow. There were three big red hearts on them, too. It was definitely girlie and groovy. It had an old striped carpet that didn't match and a disco-ball light hanging from the ceiling. It was an eight-by-ten room with two beanbags, two inflatable chairs, and a few shelves filled with old games like Cootie and tons of new CDs.

There was also lots of funky, homemade jewelry — so cool! It was a happy place; I couldn't complain.

From the looks of things, Molly and Marina were okay. I had to give them a fair chance.

So I chatted with the best friends, making one very obvious observation. They shared a brain. Now, in my more than 365,000 days, I've been close to more people than I can possibly remember. I take that back — I never forget people, even though I might get them all mixed up. But I can't say that I have ever been joined at the hip, shoulder, and ponytail with someone. I was in love once, but I am just too independent to share *everything*! I do realize that not everyone can be — or even wants to be — as free-spirited as me. And that's totally okay. Looking at these two, though, I wasn't sure that Molly could breathe without Marina in the same room, and vice versa. No one asked me, but there was no way that could have been good.

This assignment, like most, was going to have its challenges — that was clearer than a crystal ball.

I put my thoughts and opinions aside for a second and told Molly and Marina to think hard about what they really wanted. How could their lives improve?

"Mine would be better if I had my own house and Molly could move in with me. Could you help me build one?"

"No, next question." I don't do hard labor unless it's *absolutely necessary*.

"I would really like for us to do even better projects in our art class," Molly said.

"Now *that's* something I can help you with." I started to ask them if they'd ever been to Le Louvre in Paris — and if they'd ever heard of a great painter named Paul Cézanne. He was my main man! You should've seen the fingers on that kid. He could draw anything he saw. I helped him go through a breakup — he used painting to cope. I smiled just thinking of him. But I decided to keep my story to myself. When I'd said, "Cézanne," I got nothing but blank stares.

"Wait a minute, Molly," Marina said. "There's one thing we really, really want more than anything. You know what it is. Think hard."

"Hmmm. To marry best friends one day who are as close as we are?"

"Yes, but more than that . . . Who do we hate?"

"That's easy! Kristy and Keri! Wait. . . . I've got it! I've got it! Let's wish that we are better at absolutely everything than they are."

"Yes! And we want to win the art competition!" Marina added.

Well, that was doable, but I didn't want to encourage them to be mean to other girls. Of course, I could be mean if I wanted to — it's just frowned upon in the genie world. If you help someone do something really bad, you get kicked off the genie council — a fate no girl would wish on anybody.

I don't know how word gets out, but we genies hear about everything other genies do. You'd think what I did with my masters would be private. Oh, but no! My head started to hurt because this assignment was going to be sticky enough. For example, how was I going to explain that I had two kids to answer to? That I was accidentally found and hadn't followed a calling of my own? None of this was going to look good on my résumé.

Back to the issue at hand. I said to the girls, "Okay, I told you I can't do mean things. So tell me exactly what your problem is with these Kristy and Keri girls."

They told me everything. That Kristy and Keri were always buying the same outfits, after Molly and Marina bought them first. They were always taking Molly and Marina's ideas, then pretending to make them better, which of course could never happen. They were also known for saying bad things about M and M so their teachers wouldn't like them.

"This one time, when we were little — " Molly started.

Marina finished, " — Keri sat right behind Molly in first grade and cut her ponytail off! Then she said it was an accident. Yeah, right!"

"You wouldn't believe them," Molly said. "You wouldn't!"

"Every year they spread a different rumor about us and all of the kids in our class make nasty comments. It's gone on since we were in nursery school," Marina quipped.

"Yeah!" her friend chimed in.

Whew, this conversation was raising the roof on the beach clubhouse!

"In kindergarten — "

"— they told everybody that we were experimental humanoids. Everyone was afraid of us for two whole weeks." Marina didn't even stop talking to take a breath! "Then, in first grade, according to them, we were Martians. Last year, they said we were really Siamese twins separated at birth."

"They're so stupid," Molly said.

"Yeah, why would they say that when I'm black and she's white? Hello! Anyway, it doesn't matter. They keep doing all kinds of really mean things."

"Don't forget to tell Genny about the twins," Molly said.

"Oh, yeah! That was the worst!" Marina's forehead veins were throbbing out.

"I wouldn't say it was worse than the bathroom incident," Molly added.

"Molly, *yes* it was," Marina huffed. "Anyway, me and Molly liked these twin boys who were tourists. So we were on the beach just making friends with them. Well, Keri and Kristy saw us having lots of fun, and when we weren't around one day, they told our guy friends that we had just escaped from a reform school for witch-wanna-bes. The twins thought we ate cats and stuff!"

"It was terrible. We love cats," Molly said.

"So our big chance to settle the score is coming up," Marina said. "They are in our art workshop. We all have a final project to do — we want ours to be much better than theirs."

"Trillions of times better!" Molly added.

"Whoever wins the competition also gets to be in charge of the art booth at Lobster Fest in three weeks. We want to do all of that. We want them to eat our sand."

Oh, my. As long as we completed their wish in a healthy, girl-power kind of way, this would be fine. But not-so-good intentions? Now that's something that always worries me.

Chapter 6
"Oooh, Those Best Friends..."
by Molly and Marina

Genny is like a movie star — think Drew Barrymore. She's eccentric, very vintage, but *très* cool. We learned that word *très* from her, because she's French. But you can't really tell — it's not like she has an accent or anything. She says she's been in so many countries and has had so many accents she can't keep them all straight anymore! She knows a lot about everything. She was telling us how she met this little boy named Shakespeare — and she recited some famous lines that she swears he stole from her. She kind of blows us away because she's just so smart. We think it might be cool to be teen geniuses, but like we said earlier, school isn't exactly our favorite thing.

We do claim to have excellent imaginations

though — and we put them to use when we convinced Genny to help us with our one true wish. She wasn't sure that getting back at Kristy and Keri was a good idea. All we wanted to do was beat them in art class. Was that getting them back? Oh, we guess it is. But don't people who have done mean things to you since you were three deserve a taste of their own medicine? They talk behind our backs, tell everyone we're, like, ditzy. And they always show up at the same movie we're going to just so they can throw Dots at us. How childish, right? Sure, we complain, but just to each other and to Justin. Mostly we deal by keeping to ourselves. We never retaliate — not until now, anyway.

When it all comes down to it, Kristy and Keri have been jealous of us forever. Not to brag, but we are supercool. We always wear the cutest clothes because we have great taste and style sense. We also do a lot of neat things because our parents let us. We are allowed to go to the mall on our bikes if we want to. But more than anything, we have our own beach clubhouse and no one else does. We also have each other — and we never, ever fight.

But who cares about their reasons anymore? We're tired of all of it. We've sat back for way too long and let them walk all over our reps. Watch out, world! Molly and Marina are getting some 'tude!

After hearing our anti-K speech, Genny believed us. We were sure she thought Kristy and Keri needed to learn a little lesson. She said she'd help us teach them. But she also said we had to want to win that art competition for our own satisfaction as well. That was the only way she'd agree.

We said sure, that sounded cool. We *did* want to win anyway.

We finally started to figure out one thing about our strange new genie friend. As much of a brainchild as she is, the truth is that she's just thirteen like us. We could totally tell. She wasn't above complaining about a few of the people she's met in the past. Like, it doesn't sound like she was too into that dude named Napoleon or something. But more than that — for a really old thirteen-year-old, she was up on all of the latest songs. She knew every single word and sang with us. Plus, her dance moves were to die for. She also scored major points when she complimented us on our new tank tops.

Anyway, the point is that we like Genny. And she actually seems to like us, too. We are happy! Like we said before, we don't have friends other than each other — well, Molly's cousin Justin doesn't count. We hang out with him because we have to. Speaking of that boy, Justin invaded our space the day we got to know Genny — ending our fab conversation. He walked in the door, with his grubby beach shorts and flipflops on.

"So, what are you two dorks up to today?" he asked. Genny and her kitty poofed back into the bottle, which we hid under a beach blanket. We missed her already!

"Can't you see we're busy?!" Molly said.

"I'm busy, too — I just thought you might like to actually come out of this clubhouse and hang out with me on the beach. You know, you *can* be social sometimes."

"Just go away, Justin," Molly told him. "We've got major planning to do."

Chapter 7
"I Love Him."
by Marina

Why, oh, why did she send him away? I wondered as Justin left the clubhouse. I wasn't sure what had been happening inside of me over the last couple of months, but every time I saw Justin, my insides went sparkly. His green eyes were becoming beautiful. His jokes were actually funny. When he smiled at me — which was a lot lately — I went weak.

My undying love is becoming embarrassing.

I don't know how to tell Molly that I am in love with her cousin.

It's the only secret I've ever kept from her. Ever.

Chapter 8
"Oh, Come on ..."
by Molly

I felt bad for sending him away, but he was getting on my nerves.

Now, don't get me wrong, I usually don't feel guilty for dissing Justin, considering all of the pranks he pulls on me. I only felt a teensy bit evil about it because I knew Marina wanted him to stay.

She is so see-through.

I can totally tell she's got a crush the size of Maine on my cousin.

I think it's adorable!

Chapter 9
"I Don't Need This."
by Genny the Genie

Oh my goodness! Oh my goodness! This has been the worst week!

First of all, I don't feel one hundred percent good about my new girls' wish. I just hope I can show them that rivalry is ridiculous and make them happy at the same time. I have to admit, I don't like the sound of those girls Kristy and Keri. But then again, I haven't met them. I make it a point not to judge people before I talk to them face-to-face. But sometimes things just don't work out that way. Like today . . .

There is a genie girl I've never laid my eyes on, and I can't stand her! I can't help it. I hate her!

Wanna know why? What kind of girl would have the nerve to go around talking trash about me? This chick is a *brand-new* genie — she has some nerve to criticize me. I've done more good in this world than she can even imagine. I don't do things perfectly — or by the book — and I'm working on that. But I don't need some witchy new girl going around ripping me to shreds. She hasn't even met me! She doesn't know a thing about me.

She doesn't even deserve to be a genie, as far as I'm concerned. But a crazy person somewhere thought something was special about her. See, she's the Year 2000 Genie. While genies are crowned all the time, only the select, very famous few are crowned on the thousand-year marks. There have only been three of us in all of history. The first one was tapped on the Year 0 — she was called the First Genie. Sadly, she couldn't take the genie life — it does get really lonely sometimes! — and gave it up right before I was tapped. I always wanted to talk to her. She could've given me such good advice. But she chose to become human — she died the same day as her very best friend. So sad! As for me, I was in all kinds of trouble in France when I was thirteen — it's a long story. I'm just way too opinionated for my own good. Anyway, I was given the option to become a witch. That just didn't seem right for me, though, so I said no way. Meanwhile, while the old wizard was trying to figure out what to do with me, he started to dig me an awful lot. It was the Year 1000, so a special genie was needed. He decided she would be me.

Needless to say, a girl was crowned when the Year 2000 came around. She's the one who made my life crazy today. Her name is Rebecca. She's from Texas. Guess what she did? She sent out a mass genie-mail that says I am no good. She says my genie-ing is pitiful, and that I break every single rule. How dare she?! She hasn't been around long enough to even know the rules!

I don't know how these things get around, but she's already flapping her mouth and telling the whole genie world that I have two masters. But, as you know, I didn't do it on purpose! She's not talking about how great my track record is. *Nooo!* Instead she's just demolishing me, paper-shredder-style. Plus, she says I am helping girls do mean things. What? Is she trying to get me kicked out? She has no idea what kind of situation I am in. Plus, I'm a pro — I won't do mean things!

I know what I'm doing. Hmph!

I'm so mad. I am about to lose my mind. Every hair on my head is burning. If my pony-tail thins out over this, I swear I'll . . .

Now look what has happened. I'll start hating her, and all of the genies will hear about that, too! We're not supposed to get involved in these kinds of things. We're not supposed to hate, love, or get attached. We are supposed to be a forever happy and carefree bunch. And most of the time, that's exactly how I am. But the more years you do this, the harder it gets to push back your feelings. Rebecca from Texas is just too new to know about any of this. She doesn't miss her family and friends yet because they're still alive. She just needs to wait. One day she'll realize that she has outlived them all. She won't know a single nongenie soul except for her kid customers. She'll feel all alone. That's the first emotion. Others follow. Believe me, I know. I've had 'em all. Oooh, if she only knew what I've been through. Grrr.

Anyone who tries to ruin my rep is going to get it from me. I wish I could find out where that genie is. I tell you, I'd get ahold of that bottle of hers, shake it, and show her who is boss around this world.

Oooh, she'd better not mess with *moi*.

Chapter 10
"Ha-Ha! We're Going to Beat Them."
by Marina

Boy, genies can be testy sometimes. For the first day, we talked and laughed. But something definitely seemed wrong. She wouldn't come out of her bottle. But we heard her in there. She was making lots of growling noises. We decided we better just leave her alone.

It occurred to us that we still didn't have a good idea for an art project. We had already been to the mall, to the beach, and to art class. We'd even found a genie! Finally, we came up with a killer idea. We decided which project would help us win control of the Lobster Fest booth. We planned to paint a picture of the lighthouse on York Beach using nail polish. We were going to make it very abstract — using the hottest shades and sparkly colors. Now, that was going to be creative and cool! Score! We were so excited to get some tips from Genny. We knew she could help us win.

We jumped up and down. The only problem was, we'd have to learn to draw. We can paint like pros — just look at our nails. But we don't know the first thing about drawing the shape of a lighthouse. What if it was really hard? That's what genies are for!

Talk about excited! Having that idea was the best thing that's happened to us since we found Genny.

Then Justin had to walk into our clubhouse and end the whole planning session. I can't say I minded all that much — but I sure hoped no one could tell.

"Hey, I just thought I'd see what the twins are up to today," he said as he brushed his gorgeous long surfer hair out of his face.

"We can't tell you!" Molly said. We giggled until our guts hurt. Why that was funny, I don't know. But it was.

"Did I miss something?"

"No, no. We're just working on our art project," I said, smiling — make that *beaming* — at him. "We came up with a prizewinning idea, if we do say so ourselves!"

"We did, Justin! We did! You'll be so impressed."

"What? You're going to turn Molly's Lance scrapbook into a wall design?"

"Actually, that's not a bad idea," Molly said. "But no — it's much cooler than my scrapbook."

"Molly, did I hear you right?" I asked her.

"Oh my God! I think you did!" she yelled.

"So what's your project — tell me yours, and I'll tell you mine," Justin said.

"Ewww! That sounds gross," I replied. I get so embarrassed around him lately.

"Well, it's a — " Molly started to say.

"SSSHHH! You can't tell him or anybody what our plan is! Are you crazy? What if he blabs it to someone!" I was appalled. That was top secret, even to my dream beach-dude, Justin. Molly and I don't share anything we do, and we weren't going to start now.

"It's not a big deal," Justin said.

"I guess it is," Molly said. "It's a secret, and that's final."

"Anyway, it's not like I'd tell Kristy and Keri!" he said.

We screamed at the mere sound of their names. We put our heads in our hands. Justin knew we didn't even like to *think* about them in our sacred beach clubhouse. (Unless, of course, we were sharing our story with Genny — but he didn't need to know about that.)

"Calm down, calm down," he said all mischievous and laughing. We didn't like the way he always found us funny. We didn't like the way he seemed to consider us his entertainment.

"Really, you two . . . Kristy and Keri aren't that bad."

We screamed again — this time adding some "Ewwws!" and "Ickys."

"I heard just the other day that they wanted to make friends with you two — and me as well," Justin said. "I wouldn't mind being friends with them, especially Kristy."

"You know you can't trust anything they say — they probably just want to spy on us. You know, figure out what our art project is," I said.

"Oh, come on." Justin shook his head. "You are the most paranoid girls I've ever met. I think you need to give them a chance."

"You need to march out that door right now!" I said to him, mad as I could be. "We think you just better leave." Of course, I didn't *want* him to leave, but how could I say *that*?

"You two give me a headache," he said, and out the beach clubhouse he went.

Chapter 11
"Let's Do Things Right."
by Genny the Genie

I was ready to stay in that bottle for two whole years — or maybe longer. Sometimes it's best to hide from the whole world when you're feeling more like sneaker slime than a good-natured genie. What was I supposed to do? Come out and tell my masters that I was having problems with another genie? That I wished bad hair and skin on her for the rest of her very long life? That wouldn't go over well in Molly and Marina's current situation.

So I adjusted my mood — I came out with a fake smile and cheerful attitude. Sometimes if I make myself act all happy, I really start to feel that way. Luckily, Molly and Marina cheered me up, too. I had to laugh when I saw at least two hundred bottles of nail polish covering the floor of the tiny pink beach clubhouse. They were collecting every shade they could — only the gods knew why.

"What is going on here?" I asked.

"We're having a blast! We're so glad you're back," Marina said. With them, everything was "we," never I. *That* was a little strange, if you ask me. But no one asked me . . . so for once, I bit my tongue.

"Where have you been?" Molly asked. "We really missed you!"

See, that "we" thing again.

"I was, um . . . I was really tired," I explained. "I always get that way when I have a new assignment. Didn't you hear me snoring? I'm really bad about that. Good thing I'm not staying in your bedrooms!"

"Actually, we thought we heard growling. You're, like, ferocious in there — or maybe your kitty is."

"That was just snoring, I swear."

I think I convinced them that I was in a good mood. It wasn't hard to do — they were wrapped up in their own world — the art project and nail polish. Now, I have to give these two some credit. I'd never met a set of girls with a more contagious, carefree vibe. They weren't the brightest lights in all of Maine, but they didn't try to be. They didn't really try to be anything but themselves. They seemed to be happy with life exactly as it was — even if it wasn't all that deep. I really dug them for that.

Plus, they made me smile. They laughed at everything — and didn't take anything too seriously. Well, I take that back — they *did* get all in a knot over Kristy and Keri. When that subject came up, they were like water bursting out of a dam.

"Listen, about your wish," I said, not wanting to cause a flood of freak-outs. There was no doubt I was having second thoughts about helping them settle a score of rage and rivalry.

"Yeah, we have some great ideas! You just *have* to help us."

"Uh, well." I paused. "I don't know if this is such a good plan to have. I've been getting some flak from my genie colleagues."

"Coll-whos?" Molly asked.

"Okay, okay," Marina said. "Just make our project beat theirs. We won't get into all of the rest right now." She gave Molly a nudge.

Okay, fair enough. I can definitely do an art project wish — minus the rivalry.

"Fine," I agreed, not wanting to think too much about things, either. So I just listened while they came to life, telling me all about the nail-polished lighthouse painting. I had a hard time holding back my giggles. I just *knew* it wouldn't work. I didn't want them to see me lose it, so I turned around and pretended to adjust my ponytail. Yes, I give them credit for

44

being zany and creative, but the artistic merits of painting with nail polish were definitely questionable. I tried to be gentle.

"Let's work with your idea," I said. I was worried that they'd look disappointed, and they did. I could see their faces scrunching up, and whining was sure to follow. I thought fast, and boy, was I lucky when something came to me. It wasn't anything genie-us, but I hoped it would put us on the prizewinning track. Now, for the next part. I decided I'd become human to analyze this sitch. (Okay, okay — I needed an excuse to do it anyway.)

Here's the deal when I'm human. . . . First of all, other people can actually see me — not just my kid masters. That's fun because it's really weird being alone and transparent all of the time. But my favorite part is that I get to feel like real teens do, too. It's the only time when my emotions can really take control of me. As a human girl, I can experience extreme excitement, happiness, even sadness. As a genie, those things are dulled — it's business as usual. That happens to protect us genies — if we get too involved, we can get very hurt. After all, we have to leave in twenty-eight days! The problem is, I *like* to be involved. So you can see why I'm not supposed to morph into a person. It's mega-bad because when you're a human being for a while, you can be tempted to leave the genie practice altogether. But for me, it's just lots of fun. I do it on the sly whenever I can. And hey, I was doing it for the good of this assignment. You'll see. . . .

So I stirred up some dust and wiggled my nose three times. Then I shook my hips for two whole minutes. With a final tug of my earlobe, I became human. It was definitely dramatic. Lights flickered, and a strong, cold breeze whipped through a five-foot radius. All of the major magic-show-type of pyrotechnics occurred, too. It was pretty wicked — figuratively and literally. And when it was all over, you wouldn't believe how incredibly alive I felt. I couldn't wipe the smile off my face — especially when my belly began to growl. I love being a hungry human! (Genies do get hungry, just not too badly. It's just not the way our systems work.) The munchies took over.

The girls were totally wide-eyed. They went, "Cool dude!" and *ooh*-ed and *aahed*. They couldn't really tell a difference in me before or after — not in how I looked or anything. The only way I was different to them was that I had become just like any other regular kid. They could hug me and touch me. Before, I was a lot airier, and harder to squeeze and poke. I went from ghostlike to real as duck soup. (Oh, I guess no one eats that anymore. You don't know what you're missin'!)

"Let's EAT!" I said, while they were smiling and speechless at the miracle they had just witnessed. "We're going to a pizza joint. I need some food to think."

We were stuffing our faces while we threw scraps to Catfish outside. He wasn't allowed in the restaurant. I don't get it — why are people so anticat this century? I need to take up the cause of cat discrimination.

Anyway, people were staring at Molly and Marina. I think it was because they had me with them. I heard the owner of the restaurant ask them where they picked up a third wheel. "We never dive with anyone but us!" Marina explained. Of course, the extra attention made us all turn red and giggly. Then we took our piping-hot pie to our too-cool table. We ate and threw pepperoni at one another. Talk about a good time! Whew! To my surprise, Marina could make louder slurping noises with her straw than even I could. Boy, it was hard to think straight with all of that fun going on. So when we finished, I brought up the whole reason why I was there in human form.

"Where do Kristy and Keri hang out?"

They gasped. Their eyes filled with terror. It was as if I had burned down their clubhouse.

47

"Why did you have to mention them?" they asked at the same time.

"You're not going to be genie-friends with—?!" Marina freaked.

"Come on," I said. What drama queens! They were more emotional than Norma Jean was. (You know her as Marilyn Monroe!) Sheesh. "I just want to see what their art project is. . . . You know, do a little genie spying. I couldn't get the full details from the beach clubhouse — so, well, I had to get out and get to work!"

They high-fived. They really liked my idea — I didn't know if it was a good thing to do. But I didn't know how else to help them win this art contest. Nail polish just wasn't going to cut it, especially if the other kids were supercreative. And I've seen what kids are capable of — they're *artistes*!

"They're always in the art lab," Molly said. "We don't know what they're working on because we refuse to go in there."

"You don't have any clue what they do?"

"No!" Marina said. "We'd die before we'd hang out with them!"

"Well, then . . . " I told 'em to point me in the direction of that art lab. I have to admit, I had double intentions. Sure, I was going to scope out their project. But I also had to find out if Kristy and Keri were evil — for myself.

Chapter 12
"I'm Naughty."
by Genny the Genie

Yes, I'm guilty!

I admit that part of the reason I decided to spy on Kristy and Keri was because I wanted to be human. I haven't been doing that for hundreds of years. It's such a no-no. But I did it when I was with Nadia, and it felt so good!

Still, though, there was more to it than that. In order to figure out if I could even take on the assignment in good conscience, I had to see if K and K were really bad like M and M said they were. I couldn't continue on a path to deliberately ruin them if they weren't rotten girls. All I needed was for Rebecca from Texas to hear about *that*.

The other thing is, I did want my masters to do well in that art class. They have so much potential they're not even aware of — they never tap into their IQs. I was determined to show them how to do that, if I did nothing else.

But where to start? I was stumped. To be honest, I have no idea what kids do in art classes these days. Last time I went to one, they were weaving garden baskets and making kitchen pans out of clay. I am sure times have changed. So I needed to get a feel for what Molly and Marina were up against.

I made M and M stay home from class that day. They cheered because that meant they'd get to watch *Oprah*. I went to the class in their place.

Did I tell you how much fun it was to be human? Sorry, I guess I did. But yippee! The only bad part was I had bite marks all over my arms. Catfish is really against me breaking the no-human rule. Thankfully, I had a Q-Tip for him.

Everyone stared at me when I walked into class — I can't tell you how good that felt since hardly anyone ever sees me. I told the teacher, "Molly and Marina have the flu — I'm Molly's cousin, and she asked me to take notes for them." I got some weird looks, but my little white fib worked. Luckily, Justin was nowhere in sight.

Class was amazing! What a nice change from the genie-mail and the world's same-old, same-old satellite stations. I loved it — but I did have a little trouble with the oil pastel crayons. They were so much fancier than stuff we had in the tenth century. I had never seen anything like them! I started drawing little colorful flowers — the kind that little Paul Cézanne taught me to draw — all over my wooden desk. That's when the art teacher threatened to throw me out. Then he took a closer look. He said, "Wow, Genny. I think you'd better come back to class tomorrow. You're something special."

I felt so great! If only I could go back the next day . . . I'd give up my geniehood! Well, not really. (Uh-oh, I hope no one heard me think that.)

I was having so much fun that I didn't even notice when class was over. I was toiling away at a project — on paper this time — and I noticed that everyone was gone. Thank my Throttle that I heard noises in the room next door. There were a few kids in there, hard at work. The this-close girl-pair had to be Kristy and Keri.

I couldn't tell they were bad by looking at them. I mean, they were laughing and touching each other's arms the same way Molly and Marina do. I heard them talking about the same things, too — cutie boys, movies, even the same music M and M dance to. I just couldn't tell that they were evil. Then they did something *ooooh* not-so-nice.

I sat down at the desk next to the one they were sharing.

"Excuse me," one said.

I looked up. I'm always a little scared in human form because I'm not quite myself. I'm paranoid that something is strange about me.

"You're friends with Molly and Marina, right?" one of the K's asked.

"I guess so," I said, trying to play it supercool.

They gave me an eat-my-ponytail look, picked up their stuff in a huff, and walked right out of the room. I realized that they disliked me just because I was friends with M and M! Oh my, that *was* mean. I started to feel rather spunky. Despite myself I yelled, "Hey, can you tell me where the deep end is? I think I just found the shallow one."

They walked back and flipped the palms of their hands up in my face. I'd never seen that done before and was confused. Was that some sort of put-down? Then they stuck their tongues out — I knew that one — and walked away again. I started giggling because they looked so silly. They were wiggling their backsides in time with each other. I didn't mean to laugh out loud, but it was hilarious. They looked like Catfish trying to show me he was tough. Well, he isn't — and they weren't, either. I think my amusement made K and K even more steamed.

Oh, I almost forgot! I didn't even see what their art project was! What a space cadet I can be! But since they were so private with it, I figured it was what they were carrying out of class. I had to think fast. I had a couple of bucks in my pocket that Molly and Marina had given me in case I got hungry. Of course, I was famished.

"Oh, Kristy, Keri! I think you forgot something."

They turned around and looked at me.

I pointed to their desk, where I had slickly slipped three one-dollar bills. I said, "Unless you don't mind if I keep your money."

They were definitely confused, but there was no way they were leaving cash on the table. Together, Kristy and Keri strutted back to their desks to get it. I blew hard in the dollars' direction, and they fluttered to the floor. K and K shuffled around looking for the moolah and cursing at me. They said some really mean things, like, "Get a haircut," and "Your barrette is so nineties." I was just about ready to get all huffy — and tell them to zip it. But then, I got a glimpse.

Oh my goodness! That art project was super-mega-amazing. I almost hated them just because I could tell they had so much talent.

Well, that and I couldn't help but be mad about their catty comments! If they only knew who gave me my ruby barrette . . .

I stared at their artwork for just another second. Oh my goodness! Oh my goodness! What I saw blew me away. These chicks were artistic!

I raced out of that workshop. Not because I wanted to avoid another confrontation, but because I had to get to work. Molly and Marina were going to need more than just a little help.

Chapter 13
"So What!? The Mona Lisa Is for Losers."
by Marina

"You think our nail polish project is — what did you call it?" I yelled. "Molly, it was your idea!"

She looked hurt but defiant. She said, "No, it wasn't."

Genny interrupted us, swearing up and down that she didn't mean anything bad by that, but how else were we supposed to take such a comment?

"You just went to class, saw Kristy and Keri, and decided to shun us forever!" Molly said.

"Yeah, you're probably working for them now," I added.

"Dead lizards! I am not!" Genny was all worked up since she'd gone back into genie form. We didn't know what to think about that.

"Then what is wrong with nail polish?" Molly asked.

"Nothing — when you put it on your nails. But as far as this project is concerned . . . Well, I don't know how to say it without you two getting all steamed. But nail polish and lighthouses just don't go together."

"They, like, don't?" I said. "I thought it was just supercreative."

"It is, it is. But I saw Kristy and Keri's project . . . and we have some work to do."

"Pass us the paper bag! We need oxygen!" I said.

"Is it good?" Molly asked.

"It's brilliant," Genny explained. "I don't know how they did it, but they're drawing and painting a wall-sized version of the Mona Lisa."

"That weird smiling woman?" Molly asked.

"Uh, yes. The weird smiling woman," Genny replied as she shook her head.

"That doesn't sound cool to us," Molly said.

"I didn't say it was cool — it's just amazingly good. They did her in the neatest colors — fuchsia, turquoise, chartreuse."

"Oh, no."

That was definitely disappointing news.

We kept asking Genny what she thought of Kristy and Keri. We were dying to know whether she liked them or not. She wouldn't give us a straight answer, though. But she did say they gave her their ultra-snotty, talk-to-the-hand gesture. They do that to us all of the time. Can you imagine, though? They did that to someone they didn't even know — just because Genny's our friend. Now, Justin *had* to be lying when he said they wanted to be friends with us. What was up with that?

We felt bad because it was our fault that our genie got harassed in art class.

"Don't worry about it!" Genny said. "I have fried bigger fishes than them!"

She kept changing the subject — she didn't want to talk about Kristy and Keri. She was constantly looking over her shoulders like she was scared someone might hear her. That was weird because no one but us can get into our beach clubhouse.

"I want to talk about this project," she insisted. "You two definitely know how to dress. I haven't seen such cute, put-together thirteen-year-olds before."

"Really?!"

"You mean it?"

Nothing Genny said could have made us happier! We prided ourselves — and spent thousands of seconds — on putting together awesome outfits.

"So I was thinking," she said, "that you could

help me design some beautiful outfits, and I can teach you to make them."

"*Make* them?" Molly gulped.

"We are definitely good at *wearing* them," I said.

"And buying the absolute best stuff at the mall," Molly added.

"So you'd be great," our genie said while she scratched her head. She made a few squeaking noises, wiggled her hips, and clapped her hands three times. Then, *poof*! She disappeared in a cloud of smoke.

"Molly, where did she go?"

"That's, like, more radical than the Screamin' Demon at Great Escape."

"Uh, *yeah*! Molly, did you put something in my low-fat *latte*?" I asked.

"No!"

We heard a lot of whirring around in Genny's bottle. We got really nervous. The whole clubhouse started to shake! We held each other. What if it blew up while we were in it?! We couldn't take more than about two minutes of this; the room was filling with dust. We started screaming for Genny.

Thank ohmygod! She reappeared. Her hair was a total mess — kinda how mine gets after my mom takes me for a drive in her convertible.

"I've got it!" she said, smiling. Her clothes

were sooo dirty. We asked her if she wanted to borrow some of ours. We always keep emergency cutie-pie outfits in the beach clubhouse. She put some on and started talking.

"If you want to — you're going to win that contest, hands down."

We double high-fived, that news made us so happy. We didn't care how; we just wanted to win.

Then she went back into her bottle and grabbed needles, thread, and a sewing machine. She had a lot of papers in her hands that looked like they were falling apart.

"What is all of that?"

"These are patterns for some really cool dance costumes from the last one hundred years. Use these for inspiration, and we'll make up a modern one. Ours will make the clothes on MTV look dull. I'll help you — I know you can do it."

We weren't sure — we told her we didn't know how to sew.

"Brother!" she said. "What did you do before ready-made clothes?" She paused a moment and added, "After we do this together, not only will you know how to sew, you'll also be able to make all of your own clothes. It's not that hard — not when I teach you, anyway."

Now that sounded like a plan!

Chapter 14
"I Couldn't Believe My Eyes."
by Genny the Genie

Boy, did I put them to work! First, just to show M and M how easy this would be, we set out on a mission to make a pair of really simple shorts. They cut the pattern in five seconds flat — well, Molly took about five minutes, but that was okay.

"Are you going to show us how to use the scissors?" she asked while Marina chop-chopped away. Marina already had a pile of fabric laying around her feet. I wondered, *How did she know what she was doing*? I guess it didn't matter; she was going at it like a pro. She was not one bit patient, either. She grabbed the material from Molly and started working on it herself. Molly grabbed it back and said she'd figure it out. Of course I went over to help her.

She kept turning the square of cotton material back and forth, trying to figure out which side was the front. Then she started cutting away. I looked a little closer and walked over to her. "Molly, honey," I said as gently as I could. "You need to cut the khaki material, not the paper the pattern is on."

"Oh," she replied.

Marina sewed on the waistband. I swear, I didn't even have to go over there and show her how. Of course, she was putting it on backward, but that wasn't a total disaster. "Marina, wait a second," I said.

She looked up. I noticed tons of tape were stuck to her skirt. The fabric marker was sticking out of her hairdo. She looked so cute. I wished I had a camera. I smiled at her and told her how to fix the waistband.

"Ooops!" she said as she took out her stitches. She was really intense and set on getting it right.

Molly, on the other hand, was struggling to thread a needle. During one noble attempt, she jabbed the pin into her index finger. "I'm dying, I'm dying!" she screamed as she ran around in circles, blood drops dripping down her wrist.

Marina didn't even look up at her, she was so into sewing those shorts. I had to go into Throttle and find a bandage. I was glad I had an excuse to escape — the whole scene made me hee-hee uncontrollably.

I returned to see Molly looking very dismayed. She was nursing her fingertip, and Marina was covered in even more thread and scraps of khaki cloth.

Marina looked at me, her black eyes sparkling, and asked, "Hey, can we make a matching headband out of this extra strip?"

"Impressive, Marina," I said. I hadn't even thought of that! "Molly, maybe you can work on that." I handed her a thimble so her finger wouldn't get poked again.

"Thanks! That's great!" Molly was happy, because she realized this would be easier to do. Marina looked peeved, like I had taken something away from her. That was weird — usually they have a totally-in-agreement, unified front. They definitely didn't look like best buds at that very second. So I took over headband duty. I whipped up two right away, and handed one to each of them.

Well, those shorts were finished in about an hour. My apprentices were very handy — well, at least Marina was. Molly needed something else to do. I thought I'd put her on drawing duty. Maybe she'd be better at thinking up the designs.

"Those look great. The Gap couldn't have

done a better job," I said. Molly wouldn't look at Marina while she beamed.

"I get to take them home," Marina announced. Molly frowned, but didn't say anything. "After all, I made them," Marina went on.

Uh-oh, trouble.

I think I heard Molly whisper, "Shut up." But Marina definitely didn't hear it, so I let it go.

This was going to be a long art project!

Boy, was I thankful when that surfer boy Justin showed up. Since he couldn't see me or talk to me, his visit meant I was officially off-duty. I quietly sat down on a beanbag in the corner of the room, petted my cat, and stayed out of everyone's way. I just watched them — they were better than a TV show.

"Justin! You have to knock before you barge in here!" Molly yelled.

"You're a competitor, and we don't want you to see our awesome art project idea," Marina said as she gave him a little shoulder nudge. I perked up immediately. Was that flirting I saw? Hmmm . . . Interesting.

Molly then grabbed him by the elbow and said, "I'm leaving. Justin, will you walk me home?" That was strange, since she usually didn't even like him all that much. I figured she was just grumpy because her day didn't exactly go perfectly.

"See you," Molly said as she strutted out the door.

Marina looked unhappy, but didn't say anything about it. "Genny?" she asked. "Can we sew some more tomorrow?"

"Sure," I said. "Next up is the killer costume."

She was quiet — which was very unlike her — and left.

Chapter 15
"What the Heck Is Going on Here?"
by Genny the Genie

When I woke up, all was well. I had spent the night reading poetry. Best of all, I didn't receive any Rebecca harassment via genie-mail. Hopefully, she hadn't heard that I'd been human — or about any other rule you could bet I was breaking. Finally, it looked like things were going my way. The only thing I needed was a nice Nutella crepe, and things would have been perfect.

I thought about how to smooth stuff over with Molly and Marina. I figured I'd spend some extra time helping Molly brush up on her sewing. After all, she wasn't *that* bad. It's just that Marina was a whiz! That girl blew me away. She was almost as good as me — and I've had a thousand-plus years to practice. I'm telling you, I am sure I've found her hidden talent.

I sat around all morning, and neither M showed up. I was so disappointed — and a little lonely. I surfed the genie-net, worked on a few wizard spells, and waited. And waited. Finally, it was nighttime. Still feeling confused and alone, I pulled on my chicken pajamas, crawled into Throttle, and fell into a deep, snoring sleep.

Thwack! Rattle, rattle!

I thought I was having a bad dream. But then I realized I was being carried away from the clubhouse!

"Throttle, you're supposed to protect me from these things!" He didn't even seem to be awake. Catfish was meowing — totally flipping out. Have you ever seen a freaked furball? Not a pleasant sight.

I snapped three times and jumped out of the bottle — looking like a sleepy, shower-needing mess.

I couldn't believe where I was. It was a girl's room — Marina's, to be exact. I knew because she was standing right there.

"Next time can you give me some notice before you make me move?" I said, highly annoyed.

"Sorry — it was an emergency," she said as she tore down the pictures of Molly that were on her dresser.

"Hey, what's going on? Don't rip Molly

66

down!" I said, very disturbed at the whole scene.

"I can never trust her again. So I can rip her down if I want to."

"I didn't think you two ever fought," I said.

"We don't — not until now anyway. But I don't think I can ever forgive her for what she's done."

"Oh my goodness! Is it bad?"

"Very bad."

"What! WHAT?!" I couldn't take it. But this explained why no one showed up all day. I thought about them battling and both being my masters. Oh my holy Throttle. This could not be happening.

"She's a blabbermouth."

"Huh?"

"She told Justin that I was in love with him. She wasn't even supposed to know about that!"

"Oh, no," I said, trying to sound really concerned. Really, though, it didn't seem like a big deal to me. Even *I* could tell Marina had a thing for him. Couldn't everyone else?

"And she told him all about our art project."

That sounded not-good, especially since the girls had agreed it was a secret. I began to feel nervous and fidgety.

"I don't believe it! Molly wouldn't!" Really, that girl didn't do anything on her own. If she ever spoke up, it was because Marina told her to. "How did you find all of this out?"

"I got a phone call from Keri."

"*Keri?*"

"Yes! She called and was being all nice to me, if that makes any sense. Then she was like, 'Good luck on your costumes for art class.' I asked her how she knew and she was very surprised. She said, 'Oh, Justin told me.' Then guess what else Keri said? She was all, like, 'He said he heard you liked him.' Then Keri told me how cute that was. That's how I found out."

That *was* bad. Very bad.

"So what did you do?"

"I called Molly! I told her what a *blank* she was!"

"Oh, boy — I mean, oh, girl. What did she say?"

"She didn't even apologize. She said it wasn't her fault that Justin knew! I said, 'Well, then whose fault is it? I sure didn't say anything.' "

"So did you fight?"

"Fight?! YES! Then I asked why she would tell Justin that I liked him. You know what she said?"

"Tell me."

"She was, like, 'Marina, everyone knows you are in love with him. I thought you'd *want* me to tell him. You know, to set you two up!' Molly said to me, 'Listen, I was doing you a favor!' A favor? I just gave her a whole bunch of pieces of my mind — then I hung up. I never want to talk to her again. EVER!"

I have to say I couldn't help but be a bit peeved at Molly, who had obviously told Justin, who had obviously told everyone — including the worst girls possible, Kristy and Keri. Oh, this is what I call a mess. But it wasn't unfixable — at least that's what I thought. I tried to be calm and cool when I said, "Well, it's okay. We can still win."

"No, we can't — Kristy and Keri will try to top us now. And I don't trust Molly enough to work with her anymore. I never want to share anything with her again!"

A bit harsh, yes. But friend fights definitely have their own dynamics.

"And the worst is that Justin knows I like him. I am GOING TO DIE OF EMBARRASS-MENT! How am I supposed to show my face again? I am so mad at her — I can't even look at her." With that, she tore a few more pics of Molly down. There went the photo of them, three years old, in pink bunny rabbit costumes. Next, the pic of them in the second grade dressed up as pioneers. Another photo of their pet gerbil and its babies went tumbling to the ground, followed by Marina's tears.

Oh, I felt bad for her. "But, wait!" I yelled when Marina ripped a few photos in half. They were the ones of Marina and Molly at the beach clubhouse, painting the walls — and each other — pink, and blowing up all of the inflatable furniture. That made me sad.

In a crying fit, Marina interrupted my thoughts.

"I hate her! She's no best friend. I order you to stay away from Molly!" Marina commanded.

I was nearly crying, too — a tough thing to make a genie do. This was worse than watching *Old Yeller*. Then it occurred to me. I still had Molly to deal with. "Marina," I started out, sniffling, "I can't! She's my master, too!" Her command was really complicated — I don't think Marina knew what kind of terrible situation she was putting me in.

"I order you to — and you have to obey me!"

Oh, those weren't the right words to say to me. Even though I felt for her, I *don't* like being bossed around, even though my kid masters do have every right to do so. I can't help it — it makes me really mad.

"I don't take orders," I snapped, despite my genie self. Of course, what I said isn't true. I am a genie, a fact she quickly called me out on . . .

"What kind of genie are you, then?"

"I'm a genie who's going right back to the beach clubhouse. Now, you can tell me what you need me to do from there — but I'm not staying here. Things are a little too hectic for me. Besides, you brought me and forgot my cat." That was a total lie. Catfish was just being quiet in the bottle — but it sounded like a great excuse to go back to the beach, if you ask me.

"DID YOU HEAR ME? I AM ORDERING YOU TO NEVER SPEAK TO MOLLY AGAIN!"

Oh, brother.

I waited until Marina fell asleep — which took a long time because she was so wound up — a complete crying crazy girl. Not that I can say I blame her . . . But anyway, I did what I said I'd do. In the middle of the night, I snuck right back into the clubhouse. I chained Throttle's handle to a post inside. I locked it with a twelfth-century padlock. No one today would be able to figure it out. And I knew if they couldn't take Throttle, then they couldn't take me anywhere I didn't want to go. I certainly wasn't going to have them kidnapping me every night! Warfare like that can go on *forever.*

Chapter 16
"I Thought I Had a Best Friend."
by Marina *without Molly*

Jenny was gone, which was not good. I really needed her. After all, I have never felt so betrayed in my whole life.

I think this is more devastating than when Molly got her braces off before I did. I felt really alone and freaklike then, but, like, at least she didn't do that on purpose. This, however, was totally *not* an accident. She must have done it to hurt me — because that's exactly what she did. I would feel better right now if I got whacked by a dump truck. Or maybe a huge tidal wave can come and sweep me out to sea. If I could just be unconscious, being stabbed in the heart wouldn't hurt so bad.

Some best friend I have. Or had. Or thought I had.

All this time, I have done everything for her. She's shy — I speak for her. She's not sure how to do her homework — I come over and help her with it. She falls in love with some dumb sitcom star named Lance, and I collect all kinds of pictures of him off the Internet. She would be lost without me! She can't even watch TV without calling me to discuss it afterward. She can't have a conversation with anyone without telling me all about it!

And this is how she repays me?

Maybe she's been planning this for a long time. Maybe she hasn't liked me for, like, a year. Call me psychic, but I've been getting a strange vibe from her ever since we found Genny. She doesn't return my phone calls right, right away. When I send her instant messages, she doesn't always write back in a flash. And worst of all, she is starting *not* to agree with everything I say. This just makes sense. She wanted to hurt me. That's it! She has been out to get me all along! If only I had figured it out sooner.

I don't think I can ever, ever forgive her. I swear, if I could, I would. Then I wouldn't have to hurt so like a knife ripping open my insides.

If she knows me at all, she could've figured out that I wasn't ready for the world to know about my thing for Justin. I mean, I hadn't even told *her*. How would she like it if I told the world that she still sleeps with a picture of Lance *under her pillow*. Hmph. And she said she was trying to help me out — that's the biggest lie I've ever heard. Now how am I supposed to face this guy who used to be my friend? He probably thinks I'm Marina the Martian. He'll probably avoid me at all costs. This is mortification.

And the art project! She knew how much that meant to me! I've been going on about it for a whole three weeks! I bet she's just mad because I'm more of a pro making clothes than she is. She's just jealous, how much do you want to bet? I can't help it that she isn't very good at it. Anyway, it doesn't matter now, it's all ruined. My secret crush *and* the art project. Kristy and Keri are going to get exactly what they want — they'll beat us. They've got the inside scoop on us. And I don't even think I could get back together with Molly long enough to finish it.

I thought this was going to be an amazing summer!

It's the worst one of my life. I've lost my best friend. And not only that, I will never trust anyone again as long as I live. Especially her.

If best friends go through a divorce, who gets the genie? *I'm* getting the genie, that's who! I'll make sure Genny doesn't like her anymore. I'll make sure that Molly knows what it feels like to be betrayed. Genny will just have to help me do it, that's all.

But for now — I can't look at another Molly picture. I tore most of them down last night. I just finished ripping the last one off of the wall. It was my favorite — we were in a photo booth in York Beach at the beginning of this summer. That weekend, I had more fun than I'd ever had in my whole life. Our parents got us our own hotel room right next to theirs. We felt so grown-up — we'd stayed up all night every night just sharing our secrets. Then we'd run around like wild girls all day long. I never dreamed then that something like this could happen. Now all of our good times are over.

I put all of the stuff Molly ever gave me into a box. Bye-bye, charm bracelet. Bye-bye, Kermit the Frog house slippers. Bye-bye, coffee mug with our pictures on it! Okay, so I kept the best friends necklace. We both had one-half of it — I wasn't ready to get rid of that just yet. Doing such a thing would make things, like, so final.

I schlepped everything down to the base-ment. I put it so far out of sight that I hoped I'd never be able to find it again. Then I hunted for a new lock, so I could keep her out of the beach clubhouse forever. After all, it's mine. I considered it ours — everything was ours — until she forked me in the heart.

I spent the night crying. Next, I wanted all of her stuff out of my room. I got all of her CDs, books, clothes, and jewelry together. I took everything straight over to her house and left it all on her front porch. I almost left my best friends necklace, but I couldn't. I don't know why I couldn't — it's not like I'll need it anymore.

Chapter 17
"I Don't Know What to Do."
by Genny the Genie

Thank the law of gravity that I got back to the clubhouse and locked Throttle up when I did. According to the rules, Molly and/or Marina can take me wherever they want. But they're not going to — I'm breaking that rule fast. I cannot handle being passed back and forth, total yo-yo style. Well, I probably could — but I just want to stay at the beach. This place is more neutral, not to mention the fact that it's so beautiful here. It's such a treat to drink Cokes by sunset. This assignment is turning out to be so sticky that I have made an executive decision that I deserve this luxury.

After all, a friend fight can be one of the most devastating things a chick goes through. It hasn't been *that* long since I got into it with my best friend in France. Or maybe it was — it would've been a good thousand years ago when my good girl buddy Virginie and I got into it over a magic blue topaz. But see, that whole thing hurt me so badly that I still remember it like it happened yesterday.

So, needless to say, Marina versus Molly definitely concerns me. They're going to wound each other deeply. And they're going to get me in big-time trouble. This is exactly why a genie is not supposed to answer to two teens at one time. I thought I was okay, because I had stumbled onto a pair of girls with one brain. Why did they have to each discover that they had minds of their own?

Believe me, nothing is easy in the genie business.

For example, Marina has ordered me not to talk to Molly. Technically, I'm supposed to obey. But how? Molly's my master, too. I had to consult the four-thousand-page rule book on this. You can guess that looking through that thing — which weighs more than me and Catfish combined — is not my favorite thing to do. I had to, though — so I flipped and flipped. It took two eternities, but I finally found it. According to genie law, I couldn't talk to or hang out with Molly until Molly ordered me to. Molly's orders can override Marina's, and vice versa.

It looks like it's a game of whoever tells me to do something first.

That is, if I obey the rules.

Ugh. What if the genie world hears about this? What if Rebecca from Texas hears about this?

Chapter 18
"How Could She?"
by Molly

Um, well, I guess I can be my own girl. I can write this without Marina's help. I guess I can do just about anything without her help. It looks like I'll have to.

She left the beaded friendship bracelets I made for her on my doorstep! What is up with that? Next thing I know she'll leave her BE FRI half of our best friends necklaces. That will really hurt me. She didn't even call me to discuss — we always used to talk about everything. I guess you don't talk about breaking up.

I don't know whether to cry or to get really, really, *really* mad. I've never been apart from Marina for more than a day before. I mean, we've been the best of buddies since we were two years old! So, yes, I miss her. I miss her terribly. But I'm also mad.

If she really cared about me as much as she always said she did, how could she not try to see my side? She didn't even give me a chance to explain everything before she hung up on me! I've tried calling her, and she keeps having her sister answer. I know she's home, no matter what her family tells me. I know where Marina is at all times.

She did leave me a long note — next to the bracelets. It said all kinds of mean stuff, like that she can't trust me. And she's seen this coming. Seen it coming? I thought we were having an amazingly fun summer! Yes, she was getting on my nerves a little more than she used to — but things were still great.

This whole situation is just getting more and more complicated. And I'm getting more and more mad. And sad.

I only told Justin that Marina liked him because he asked me point-blank. We were walking home when he said, "I think your best friend has a thing for me." He nudged my elbows until I giggled — which divulged the secret without me saying a word. So I just said, "Yeah, you're right. I think she does." I didn't want to lie because it seemed like he might have a crush on her, too. (Of course, our conversation didn't quite get that far.) I wasn't trying to spread her secrets — but come on, the boy already knew! As for our art project, I told him because I knew there was no way he'd copy off of us. He can't design clothes! Plus, I trusted him. I didn't dream he'd tell our old archenemies, Kristy and Keri. I was just as shocked as Marina was! I swear! I am sure that if Marina and I weren't fighting, we'd be double mad at him. And I am kind of peeved, but what can I do? I don't have a friend in the world. I can't exactly afford to diss my cousin. I just wish Marina knew that I'm not the horrible, bad best friend she thinks I am!

I decided I had to go to the beach clubhouse. I couldn't stand sitting in my room anymore — it was lonely without Marina in it. Maybe Genny could help me. I was so confused. I couldn't take it anymore.

On the walk over there, I got to thinking about it, though. Marina hasn't been that great to me lately. She was really mean to me when we were learning to design clothes — I can't help it if I'm not as good as she is! Plus, she bosses me around, speaks for me, and tells me how my homework isn't good enough. I never do things like that to her. I'm always super-sweet. And I have always been there for her — especially whenever she cries, which is a lot. And whenever she picks a fight with her sisters — that happens a lot, too — I always take her side, no questions asked. I drop everything — my favorite books and even my made-inheaven sitcom with Lance on it — for her crisis of the moment. She has to know that she has always been the most important thing to me. How could she not know that?

And now she wants to treat me *this* way? She wants to throw our entire friendship away? I know this is a mess — maybe I did something I shouldn't have done. But she isn't perfect, either. She can't just go around assuming that I did all of this to be mean to her. She is so unfair.

For once in my life, I'm going to stick up for myself. I'm not going to just forgive Marina overnight. I can't — I'm tired of her 'tude.

I was so upset that I started shaking. I began to run to the clubhouse. I wanted Genny.

And the nerve of that Marina! She locked me out. I looked inside. Genny was demolishing a pepperoni pizza like there was no tomorrow. She finished the last bite and yelled at me through the door.

"Molly? Is that you?"

"Yes, please let me in."

"Okay, but you have to order me to talk to you and to hang out with you."

"Huh?"

"Please, for my sanity, just do it."

Weird, but I did it. "Genny, I am telling you to let me in." It felt strange to boss someone around.

Genny looked even more stressed than I was. She looked a little mad at me, too. I started bawling — then I told her everything that happened. She was mad at Justin, I could tell. She kept going, "Oooh, boys . . . *grrr.*"

She knew exactly what to do to make me feel temporarily better. She rubbed my hair and held my hand. She put on some music and told me a joke. I smiled a tiny bit — she was helping me calm down. But I knew a few minutes later, I'd just feel bad all over again.

Losing a best friend *hurts*.

Chapter 19
"What the Heck?"
by Genny the Genie

Something's going on with that boy, Justin, but I don't know what. Aren't cousins supposed to be loyal to each other? He should not have told Molly's secret to Kristy and Keri. I don't know why she's not more mad at him. She just says that's the way he is! And meanwhile, Marina's still in love with this no good little . . .

I wish I could get inside his head. Maybe Catfish can see what's going on. Oh, kitty . . . I sent him to Justin's for a quick spy session. I just wanted to make sure he was legit.

It seems like my purpose here is getting murky. Do Molly and Marina still want to win that art competition? Are they still after Kristy and Keri? I had to sit long and hard to think about my meaning in their world. It seems like everything has been rearranged — actually, it has! Marina even took her inflatable furniture home. Where does she think I'm going to sit?

Okay, so I could still plop down in the bean-bag — and that's exactly what I did.

My brain became sore, I was thinking so hard.

But one thing wasn't neurosurgery. I had to get those girls back together. Molly without Marina was like fish without chips. Marina without Molly was like having a corn dog without the ketchup. They were both completely unhappy and lost. But the last thing I could convince either of them to do was talk to each other. Boy, I had my work cut out for me. At least my new mission was clearer than an acne pad — I had to get those two back together.

Catfish came back all raggedy and happy. I could tell he had made a little detour into a trash dump. He had chicken bones still stuck to his lips. I washed him off, reprimanded him — "Don't you know we actually have to work?" — and waited for him to tell me about this Justin kid.

Catfish used his tail to tell me what happened. He's a strange cat who's developed his own kitty sign language. And I'm the only one who can understand him. (Hey, we have a lot of time to kill inside of Throttle.)

"Slow down!" I yelled.

He stopped completely — that's the obstinate kind of animal he is. I had to pet his head and make him purr before I got a straight answer. I can help save the world, but I can't control my cat.

The furball finally told me that Justin spent most of the night on the phone. One call was with Keri, the other with Kristy.

"That's all you got?" Yep, that was it.

It wasn't a whole lot of info — but it was enough to make me suspicious of that boy beach bum.

Chapter 20
"I Don't Know What to Do."
by Molly

"This is terrible! I can't think of anything worse!" I yelled. "I'd rather have my nails ripped out one by one than go through this!"

"No, no. No, you wouldn't," Genny said. She reminded me that she had seen that happen way back when. Ewww. Anyway, she was being really helpful, and boy, was I glad to have her around. I don't know how Genny got so smart, but she was wise about friend things — at least she seemed to know exactly what it felt like.

But then she wasn't cool at all — she offered to talk to Marina for me, to clear up this whole mess. "How can I crawl right back to her?" I asked. "She even sent my friendship bracelet back. What kind of old pal would do that? I'm not just crawling back to her. I need to stand up for myself for once. If she had listened to me for one second right after all this happened, we wouldn't even be half as mad at each other. I mean, this is mostly her fault!"

"I think she was just mega-surprised and upset at first," Genny said. "When you're that worked up, you don't always think straight."

"I don't care! No, don't tell her that I miss her or anything. Even though I do. Just tell her that she's being way too mean. You tell her that I'm the best thing that ever happened to her. Tell her she'll be sorry she gave me those bracelets back."

"Do I really have to say all of that?" Genny asked.

"Yes," I said, getting spunkier by the second. "I command you to!" I couldn't believe I actually *commanded* someone to do something. I'd never done that by myself in my whole life. I admit, it felt really good. "Tell her she'll be sorry she dumped me like this. She'll be sorry she didn't give me a chance to explain." I was losing it — being sad and mad at the same time is dangerous for me.

Genny rubbed her temples. I just kept right on talking. "And when you're at her house, please get the other half of our gold best friends necklace back — it says BE FRI. I gave it to her, and I know she loves it. Tell her I want it back ASAP! I'll give her something to get mad at me about!"

"I don't know if I can do this."

"But I'm, well —" I almost backed down — taking the necklace was a little mean. "I'm ordering you to, and I, um, mean it!"

Genny went on her way, looking anything but happy. She was definitely sulking — refusing to do her nails with me while I did mine. But at least she did what I asked.

Things were happening way too fast, so I took a walk. I needed to relieve tension and I was tired of crying. I remembered the way my dad and mom used to go down to the beach with me after we'd all gotten into a no-fun family argument. So that's where I went. I was hoping to catch the sunset. I needed some peace!

I got none of that. I was sitting on a rock in the public part of the shore, and then I saw her.

Yuck.

Kristy.

Ick.

And she was walking up to me. I was just starting to calm myself down and I got all worked up again. I had to rack my brain for good put-downs — because you could bet she wasn't going to say anything nice to me.

"Hey, Molly," she said.

I looked at her with my eyes scrunched up. "What do you want?"

"Well, I heard about your art project. And — "

"Cork it, Kristy. I don't think we're even going to do it anymore." I just wasn't in the mood to get into a put-down contest with her. I decided to ignore her instead — which is what I had been doing to K and K their whole lives. Then she surprised me.

She said, "Well, I think you should."

"Huh?"

"It's really cool. I just wanted to tell you that."

At first, I thought she was up to something — then I noticed she seemed really sincere. She even seemed kinda sad. Well, at least we had that in common. I guess she could tell I was confused. Kristy just stood there for a moment looking at the sunset with me. I actually enjoyed it for half a second until I realized who I was with: Crusty Kristy. Just when I was about to tell her to beat it, she began to walk away.

"Bye, Molly. See you around," she said really sweetly.

I didn't say anything back, but I definitely didn't think she was up to something. I just didn't feel like she wanted to do anything but be nice to me. Could it be that she's an okay person without her sidekick Keri?

Chapter 21
"This Is Crazy"
by Genny the Genie

Molly is majorly mad. Marina is even madder. I am stuck smack in the middle.

What is a genie to do?

I decided to do what I was told — well, mostly.

I sent Catfish ahead of me to see if anyone was home at Marina's house. When I heard that the coast was clear, I made my move.

I didn't bother to knock or anything — not like anyone can see me anyway (I went back into genie form). I just walked right into her big white house.

"Marina?!"

"If it's Molly, then get out!"

"It's Genny."

She ran down the steps, then took me to her room.

"I was just coming to see you," she said.

"I think we need to talk."

"About what?"

"You and Molly."

"Who? I don't know anybody named Molly." She looked in the mirror, which looked so plain without best friend pictures all over it. She played with her hair. Marina was obviously nervous just talking about Molly.

"I think this has gone just too far," I said, remembering what an excellent diplomat I used to be.

"Too far? You think what she did was right!?"

"Listen, she didn't do anything. I am sure of it." Okay, so I didn't obey *all* of Molly's orders — I was just trying to improvise. I can't stand to see people fight!

"What? You talked to her? I shouldn't be surprised. Why should you obey anything I say? It's not like you're a genie or anything." She was sarcastic. I hate sarcastic.

"I *did* obey your orders, Marina. Then Molly commanded me to talk to *her*. I have to do what she says, too, you know."

"Oh, yeah . . . Like, what did she want you to do?"

"Well, to be honest, she said" — I paused — "she said . . . " I hadn't planned to do this . . . But, oh, well! "She really loves you and misses you."

"She did not," Marina said, looking sad.

"Do you miss her, too?" I asked. There, things were going much better. I am such a good mediator!

Before Marina could answer, though, the phone rang. She wiped her eyes and rushed to the phone. I thought that was a good sign — hopefully, she was waiting for a call from Molly. Oh, rainbows! I was getting happy! Until . . .

"Hi, Justin!" Marina excitedly yapped on the phone. I couldn't believe my ears — I had to wonder if they were working right, or if I needed to request new ones. She could not have been talking to *the* Justin, could she? Maybe there was a little romance in the crisp Maine air. I sure hoped so — I wanted something, *anything* happy to happen.

"What?" she said, her tone totally going in the grumpy direction, much to my dismay. "You're kidding," she continued. "No way — she would never. I don't believe it. Are you sure?"

Pause.

"So you're positive?" she asked, her voice starting to waiver. "I'm sorry." She was losing her cool — I was going nuts wondering what was up!

"I can't talk right now," she said as she plunked the phone down.

Marina began to cry. I thought she'd be happy to hear from her dream beau! But I wasn't surprised. This boy was the devil — not a dream.

"What happened?" I asked.

She cried harder. "Justin just told me that Molly was hanging out with Kristy on the beach! I can't believe it! How could she do that to me? She doesn't miss me. Tell her to forget it. I never want to see or hear from her as long as I live."

That was not the setback I needed. What was going on? I was just with Molly and she hadn't mentioned Kristy. Ugh. Was this assignment destined for doom?

I tried to calm Marina down, telling her everything was okay. I patted her back and handed her tissues. It took an hour, but she finally stopped sobbing. Whew! I was glad. I was afraid she would wind up dehydrated! I snuck away quietly, telling her I'd see her in the morning.

I didn't want to do it, but on my way out, I swiped Marina's BE FRI necklace right out of her dresser drawer. I only obeyed that part of Molly's command because I had to — what would I tell Molly if I came home empty-handed? I just hoped Marina didn't find out. I felt extra bad about it, though, because I heard Marina weeping again as she shut her bedroom door.

During my journey back to the beach, I wondered who that Justin jerk thought he was. If he only knew that he was about to wage a war with *moi*!

Chapter 22
"Now I'm Really Gonna, Like, Croak."
by Molly

I went to the clubhouse, hoping that Marina would show up. She hadn't stopped by since our fight first started. Sure, I was rip-the-moon-down mad at her, but I couldn't help hoping and praying that she'd pop in one day and everything would be back to normal — beach business as usual.

Nothing was the same, though. I was feeling crabby. It definitely didn't help for Genny to be mad at me. She hadn't said three words since I got there that morning. Has your genie ever been upset with you? It's like when your sweetest auntie — the one who's never ever mad — raises her edgiest voice at you. I didn't feel right inside.

"Will you please tell me what's wrong?"

Finally, she did — and I was sorry I asked.

Genny hurled the BE FRI half of Marina's necklace at me. Next, she threw a mean expression at me — one that pierced through my heart and almost made me cry.

"What?" I asked.

"How could you? How *could* you?"

"How could I what?"

"You know, hang out with Kristy?"

Brother. The whole world already knows about that. I hate my bo-ring small town. "I didn't hang out with her."

"Yes, you did — and the worst part is, you didn't even tell me about it. I went over to Marina's, and she was a mess over it."

"Oh, no! Kristy came up to *me*. I have no idea why. We talked for, like, three seconds. I swear!"

"I don't know if I believe you. My sources say you two were all cozy on the beach. What kind of sneaky stuff are you up to, Molly?"

"Nothing, I was just lonely yesterday. You went over to Marina's, so I went to watch the sunset. I just needed some quiet. I was shocked to see Kristy walking up to me."

"Then what happened?" She looked like she wanted to believe me, but didn't.

"I was all ready to tell her to drown herself when she told me my art project sounded really cool. Then she stood there a few more minutes and left. She was actually really nice to me, not that I trust her."

"Oh, really." Genny was wondering about something. I didn't dare ask what.

"So Marina thinks I was hanging with her?" I began to get all upset. That's when Genny finally figured out that I was not lying.

"Yes!"

"And then she must've been much more hurt when you took the necklace from her."

Genny disappeared into her bottle for about five minutes. My stomach hurt — I was a nervous wreck. Things aren't supposed to be so messed up in the summer! I couldn't even figure out how this all happened. I wanted to call Marina. I wanted to so badly. I decided I would do it as soon as I got home.

Genny reappeared. She had tons of material and even more needles in her hands. She had an armload of the latest CDs, too.

"I don't know. I'm not in the mood," I told her.

"We're starting on this art project and we're going to have a great time!"

We danced around and sang songs. I drew a few really cool versions of a costume better than anything Madonna would wear. Genny loved them all — but she chose the fluttery, most intricate one. It had beads all over the top, with a beautiful leotard and a see-through skirt on the bottom.

"You don't know this," she told me, "but you just drew an amazing costume. Martha Graham wore delicate, gorgeous outfits. And I love the way you've updated it. Just imagine your favorite female singer doing a dance number in this. She'd look like a beauty queen."

At least something was making me smile. I felt like I hadn't smiled in ten years — I was glad we worked on the project. So after I did the design, I was set on sewing. And Genny was way into showing me how. We had a great time!

I cut shapes, pinned elastic into the right parts. I chose the beads that would be sewn onto the neckline. We worked with the lace — figuring out which was the best. It was going to be beautiful!

It got dark outside, and Genny began to yawn. She said she'd have to go to bed, but that we'd get to work tomorrow. All of a sudden I was really sad. I wished Marina were with me. Usually, if we had done something really special — like I'd done today with the costume — we'd spend the night together and celebrate. But scarfing down a whole bag of Nestle's dark chocolate chips by myself definitely left a lot to be desired.

I decided for sure that I was going home, straight to the phone, and dialing up my ex-best friend.

So that's what I did. I was really nervous and happy and worried while the phone went *ring, ring, ring*.

"Hello." It was her! Marina!

"Marina?"

"Molly?" She sounded surprised, and kinda-sorta happy that it was me. Well, she did at first. "What do you want?"

"I want to talk."

"Go talk to Kristy," she said before she hung up on me.

Then the phone rang. I was so excited — I was sure Marina was calling me back. Hopefully, she really did want to work things out. "Molly," the voice said on the other line. Well, it didn't sound like Marina . . . but I thought maybe she was just upset. Oh my goodness! I was sooo wrong.

Instead, that mean voice said, "You stay away from Kristy."

I hung up immediately — I was sure it was Keri. My life was turning into *The Twilight Zone*.

Chapter 23
"Oh, Brother!"
by Genny the Genie

I couldn't even keep up with what was going on — and I'm completely accustomed to complications. So instead of sitting around waiting for either Molly or Marina to please fill me in on this friendship feud, I decided to go to art class myself. Okay, so I love art class. But I really did have a job to do, too.

Molly and Marina would be there, so would that creep Justin, and so would Kristy and Keri. I wanted to see who was speaking to who, who was giving who the evil eye. I planned to spy big-time. I was heading to their class kinda-sorta incognito. Of course, Marina and Molly could see me, but no one else could.

For the afternoon, I became special agent Genny the Genie. Well, you can't say my job is boring.

I arrived after the teacher had started talking. I stood right next to him in front of the class. I was just trying to prove a little point. Molly and Marina — sitting on opposite sides of the room — were wide-eyed. But they couldn't say anything to me. Not without looking crazy, that is. Hee-hee! I had so much fun.

"Yes, Molly," her art instructor asked while she waved to me. Everyone looked at her in a who-are-you-saying-hello-to? way. She turned red and thought fast.

"There was just a pesky *bug* flying around my desk," she said, shooting an annoyed look my way. Marina was snickering, not waving.

I took a spot at an empty desk and let Molly and Marina get used to me. Pretty soon, they were just taking their class as usual and not paying too much attention to me.

Justin looked innocent enough. He was sitting in the back of the classroom, intently working on the day's work. He wasn't up to anything that I could see.

Kristy did go over and sit next to Molly while I was watching. Molly seemed uncomfortable. She wiggled a lot in her seat, leaning on one side, and then the other. It looked like Kristy struck up a conversation that Molly couldn't ignore. I saw Molly sneak a glance back at Marina. Boy, did Marina look mad, glaring at her ex-best friend with a how-dare-you stare of steel.

Marina quickly took matters into her own hands. She got up out of her seat and sat next to Keri. Keri ate it up. They laughed and giggled in a totally insincere way — I could *so* tell that they were trying to make Molly and Kristy jealous. Meanwhile, those two genuinely seemed to be getting along.

Oh my goodness! What an interesting day in art class!

I could see part of the problem right away. Not only were Molly and Marina at each other's earrings, Kristy and Keri were, too. It kind of explained things — Molly and Kristy had something in common. Both of their best friends were mad at them, for whatever reason. So Marina and Keri retaliated by creating their own little pair.

Not good.

I stuck around while everyone walked out. Molly and Kristy were deep in conversation. They left first and fast — it didn't look like they wanted to cause any trouble. Marina and Keri were talking, too, presumably about their ex-best friends.

The most interesting thing I saw was hiding behind a tree, watching all four girls. His name was Justin. He was nodding and rubbing his chin. It was all I could do to keep from becoming human right then and there. More than anything in the world, I wanted to tell him a thing or two. It was a good thing he can't see or hear me in genie form. He would have suffered some serious verbal abuse. I learned a little something from hanging out with grumpy czars and their children.

That lowdown little dirty rat had everyone fooled. "Oh, Justin's so funny," Marina had said. Or, like Molly once told me, "He can't help how naughty he is — he's a sweet guy inside." Well, I tell you what. He sure didn't have me fooled.

As I always say, if it walks like a rat and acts like a rat, it's usually a rat.

After all of that, I had to go home to an empty pink-and-yellow house. I guessed that Molly and Marina were avoiding each other, so I would not be getting visitors. I wanted some — I just wanted to moan and vent to someone. I decided to log on to genie-mail, which usually provides the perfect outlet for such activity.

To my horror, I saw it — a mass e-mail that was sent out to everyone I know. Here is what I read:

to: genie pop
from: rebeccatex
regarding: genny1000
hi y'all. i am just writing to make you aware of

the problem genie we have on our hands. her name is genny. here are all of the rules she's broken in the last few days alone:

1. she has two masters — who, by the way, hate each other.

2. she doesn't always obey them — in fact she usually does just the opposite.

3. she — brace yourselves — becomes human whenever she wants.

i think we need to start enforcing some rules around here!

rebeccatex, the Year 2000 Genie

Oooh. How dare she! That was it! She was spying on me somehow. And she was really making me mad. She was taking all of the well-intentioned things I did and making them sound bad! She was twisting everything around. I did not need this. I couldn't think of my assignment and of this witch, too. Anyway, if my methods worked, who cared if they were questionable? I hate to see new genies get all high and mighty about the rules — especially when they've had, what?, just five or six kid assignments. She'll see how hard it gets after you've had a thousand or so — believe me, she'll see. I'd like to see her make a girl feel better in ten minutes flat going by the book. But

106

instead of getting patted on the ponytail for a job well done, this nasty chick was basically frying me at the stake. I couldn't figure out why.

Thinking about it, I didn't sleep — or snore — a wink.

Chapter 24
"At Least I'm Not So Lonely."
by Marina

Genny came to my house and stayed with me all morning. She was worried because I hadn't been stopping by the beach clubhouse anymore. I guess I've been depressed. Who wants to go there? It has too many memories.

Well, Genny convinced me. She said there was no way Molly would be there. And she said I needed to get out of my room. I fixed my hair and put on cute clothes. At least that made me feel a little better.

We were on our way to the beach when Genny started asking me all about Keri. Honestly, I didn't know her that well. But she seemed okay when she was away from Kristy. She certainly wasn't mean or anything. She was actually nice.

"The best thing is," I said, "she knows exactly

how I feel. She and Kristy got into a fight over their art project, too."

"Really? What happened?"

"Well, I guess Justin gave them some pointers on making it better, and then they fought because they wanted to do different things to it," I said. Genny was dead silent. "Justin's the one who said Keri and I should get together sometime, so we did. It's not like either of us had best friends to hang out with!"

There was a long silence. "What's wrong?" I asked her.

"I think Justin — " she started to say.

"What?"

"Nothing." With that, she totally changed the subject. She didn't want to talk about it anymore. She wanted to work on the dance costume. Genny knew just the thing to do to put me in costume-design mood. She danced around the room and put on a few of my favorite CDs. Then she got the thing out of her bottle. She and Molly had been hard at work on it.

It was a complete mess.

Even Genny admitted it. We laughed so hard. The pieces were on all crooked, and the stitches were uneven and terrible. I could see what it was supposed to be, but it looked like a first grader had gotten hold of it. Turns out, it was just Molly. "See why I needed you to come here so badly?" Genny said. She explained that Molly designed the thing like a pro — she just couldn't sew to save her hairdo.

That's where I came in. I whipped that sucker up in about two hours. It looked amazing. Genny was mega-impressed with me. She said the last time she saw talent like mine, she was with young Betsey Johnson.

"*The* Betsey Johnson?" I jumped up and down. I love clothes, so I actually knew who she was. She makes expensive, flowery, girlie dresses. They're funky and fab. I would love a few of my own, but it's not like I can get good designer clothes where I live in Maine. "You really met her?" Genny explained that Betsey had some tough challenges, but she was so positive and happy that she worked them out. And look at her today! "Oooh!" I squealed.

I think Genny waited for me to calm down before she broke the next bit of news.

"I want to turn in this art project under both of your names — yours and Molly's," she announced.

"Best friend, enemy-loving Molly? No way!"

"Wait a second, you're hanging around with Keri," Genny said.

"Only because Molly hung around with Kristy first."

"I thought you said you liked her."

"Yeah, well . . ."

"Well, then, you can't be all mad at Molly."

That made me really mad. After all of the things Molly had done, and I couldn't be mad at her? "Oh, yes, I can!" Just as I said that, I saw my half of the best friends necklace on the bookshelf. "What's this?" I turned to ask Genny. The sight of it still made my eyes fill up with tears. I wondered if I'd ever get over this.

"Oh, um," Genny stammered trying to answer me.

"I HATE HER! HOW COULD SHE! Did she make you take this from me?"

"No, I just wanted to borrow it," Genny said. I could totally tell that she was lying through her ponytail.

"Yes, she did! I know she did! She probably wants to give it to Kristy." I began to cry for a minute, and even Genny couldn't calm me down.

"Don't you dare put her name on that project. I made it look great — she didn't." I was just saying anything to be hateful toward her. That's what kind of rage I was in. "I command you — don't turn it in at all if you're going to put her name on it!"

Chapter 25
"Oh, Marina! Oh, Molly!"
by Genny the Genie

Boy, I was glad that Marina didn't find the best friends necklace until *after* I convinced her to finish the art project! I don't think I could've gotten her to lift a fingernail if she'd seen that first. Then I would've been out of luck — they never would've finished what they started. The amazing art project would have been history — my time with Molly and Marina would have been for nothing. I kicked my Throttle for not remembering to hide that gold piece of jewelry. It could have ruined everything! Sometimes I'm the ditzy one!

Molly stopped by after Marina left, and I quickly hid the dance costume. I didn't want her to see the improvements — I had told her what a great job she did. Well, she *did* do the design. Her sewing just stunk.

We sat and talked. I asked her why she was hanging with Kristy so much.

112

"Well, Justin said I should!" she answered.

I knew it! I had a feeling he was behind it. I didn't want to let her in on my suspicions until I worked out all of the details. I had no idea what he was up to — just that it was no good.

"He did, huh?" I said, not letting her figure out what I was thinking.

"Yeah, he knew I was really lonely without Marina, so he told her to say hi to me at the beach that day," Molly explained. "And the rest is history."

"But I thought she was a terrible person?"

"When Keri's not around, she's totally nice! She even apologized for everything — the name calling, the copying, the ponytail of mine that got chopped off. I'm telling you, the chick is with it. She's a really nice girl. I wish I'd gotten to know her sooner."

"Molly, do you miss Marina at all?"

"No!" she insisted, but I didn't believe her.

"Come on," I said. "Just a little?"

"I miss her more than anything, but every time I call, she just hangs up. It's so painful. Not even my I Love Lance scrapbook can cheer me up. So I just hang around with Kristy and try not to think about it."

"I think you and Marina will work it out," I said. (If I had anything to do with it, they would!)

113

"Never."

I couldn't listen to her talk about it anymore — it was just too sad. But at least I started to feel better knowing that the M and M versus K and K rivalry was over forever. I didn't have to do anything mean because my girls had become friends with the enemies. Now, my biggest problem was that they were enemies with the friends, if that made any sense. My mission was all too clear — I had to get Molly and Marina back together. Neither of them commanded this of me, but under-neath all of their pride and hurt, I knew that's what they both wanted more than any-thing. I smiled because I knew if I did every-thing just right, M and M would both be happy again.

So I gave Molly my game plan. "Well, listen," I said. "I am turning in the art project with both of your names on it."

"No, you're not! She didn't even work on it!" Well, that's what Molly thought, and I sure wasn't going to fess up. Uh-oh, my plan to get them together wasn't working. I'd have to do something about that!

"Genny. Did you hear me?" Molly demanded.

"Okay, okay," I answered. As you probably know, I didn't hear a thing. Molly's words went in one earring and out the other!

"No, I don't trust you," Molly said. "Give it to me, and I want to see you seal up the envelope."

I went into Throttle with a lot of dust and fanfare. I was trying to be showy to distract her attention from the conversation at hand. I put scraps of the old costume — the one Molly had worked on — into a big envelope. I came out of Throttle and showed Molly that her project was in there. At least, from what she could see, she thought it was. I made a tag that said, SUBMITTED BY MOLLY. I sealed it up, and said, "There you go."

"Mail it tomorrow," she commanded. "And don't sneak Marina's name onto it."

"Sure thing," I said.

Molly left, and I went straight to the art workshop. I slid an envelope under the door. It was Molly and Marina's collective dance costume — the new and improved version that Molly had designed and Marina had sewn. Whether they knew it or not, it was truly a work of art. It didn't look like teens had made it — the outfit looked totally real and professional. I didn't care what they had told me to do — or not to do — I slapped both of their names on that sucker before I sealed it up. I submitted it and strutted home.

Sometimes the best rules to live by are my own.

Chapter 26
"I'm onto Him."
by Genny the Genie

Things keep getting more and more interesting around here. Molly and Kristy were at the beach clubhouse this morning — having tons of fun. I was horrified at first because no other girl besides M and M had ever been in the small, private clubhouse. And the nerve of Molly — if Marina had found out, she would've cried and cried! But I do try to be open-minded. I'm sure she brought her new bud for a reason. I sat around silently and watched them talk. I have to say I liked what I saw.

Kristy was smart — and Molly acted like a brighter light around her. I knew she had a secret, sharp side! There was no giggling and squealing, although there was lots of talk about boys, the mall, and music. You know, the usual. These two were tight — I could tell they made a good team. They also talked a lot about losing their best friends. Since that was so super-sad, I was glad Molly had someone to lean on.

Throughout the morning, Molly made sure to smile and wink at me a lot, since she couldn't talk to me with Kristy around. I'm sure Molly was trying to be slick and show me that Kristy was cool. I knew exactly what she was up to. But she didn't need to put on a show — I already agreed. Kristy was sweet, calm, caring, and smart. I couldn't help but like her.

Still, I did *not* like who came in next.

Justin! Yuck! I wanted to crawl into Throttle and hide. But my curious side wouldn't let me. I couldn't even show how much I really despised him — I didn't want Molly to be able to tell that I wished really bad sunburn on her cousin.

He yapped with the girls, and he, too, seemed to notice how well his cousin and Kristy got along.

"I told you," he said, and my ears perked up. "You two are so much alike! I knew you'd be a good pair."

"I'm so glad you got us together," Molly said, squeezing Kristy's hand.

"But what about Marina?" Justin asked. "Haven't you talked to her?"

It suddenly dawned on me that maybe he didn't have terrible intentions.

Oh, my goodness! I couldn't believe I didn't think of it before!

Thank the maker for genie-mail! Just before bedtime, I tapped into the human system. It's simple and provincial, but you people seem to like it. I did an exhaustive search — okay, it was easy — and found his e-mail address.

I wrote him a little anonymous letter.

to: beachboy13
from: genny1000 (I used my real name, since he wouldn't know who I was anyway.)
hi, justin,

you don't know me, but i know you. i think you've been messing with your cousin molly, and her best friend, marina. i also think you're playing games with kristy and keri's friendship. this needs to be fixed asap. please tell me what you're up to. maybe i can help.

genny

Next thing I knew, I heard a "Bling!" A message popped up on my screen. I was excited to get those things you all call instant messages! And even better, it was from the boy himself.

to: genny1000
from: beachboy13
hey, who are you? you can't be marina or molly — they're not on-line right now. how did you know that i need major help?

118

to: beachboy13
from: genny1000
it doesn't matter who i am — just think of me as your guardian angel. i know you need help, and i'm here to give it to you. i just have a few questions.

to: genny1000
from: beachboy13
is this my aunt joy, molly's mom? it is, isn't it? i don't even care — just help me out.

to: beachboy13
from: genny1000
no, my name isn't joy, it's genny. i just need to know . . . why did you break all of these best friends up? was there any rhyme or reason to your madness?

to: genny1000
from: beachboy13
i didn't mean to break them up — i was just trying to get them all to be nice to each other. i was tired of constantly being in the middle of a big showdown between molly & marina and kristy & keri. it wasn't any fun. so i told myself that this summer, i'd get them all to be friends. the five of us could hang around and have fun! after all, my best friend (who's a guy) has to

go to his grandma's every summer — so i need
people to hang around with. but i didn't know
that marina really liked me . . . or that molly
and marina would fight, or that any of this
other stuff would happen. this is a mess! now
there's more fighting than ever! i've got all of the
girls apart, but i can't seem to get them back
together.

I wish I'd caught on earlier. This boy wasn't bad at all! I couldn't believe my eyes. I reread the computer screen, like, five times. I usually don't get this mixed up. Then again, I haven't dealt much with modern boys. They definitely can be different.

to: beachboy13
from: genny 1000
stick with me . . . i've got you covered.

We e-mailed back and forth for five hours. I could see why Marina liked him — he was a little charming. Anyway, it was like three in the morning, and I had to get to sleep. I needed my brain to be on full-power for all of the plotting I planned to do tomorrow.

With that boy's help, I'd have everybody hugging, kissing, and jumping up and down in no time.

Chapter 27
"I've Got It."
by Genny the Genie

Ugh. Hmph. Oh!

The book I needed was buried deep inside Throttle. It was all about how to fix things, and I knew it had a specific section on friend fights. But it was three thousand pounds heavy, covered in dust, and at the very bottom of everything I owned. I guess you can see I use my genie manuals a lot.

Getting it out made me sweaty and ruined my lip gloss. I was not happy about having to use it. Flipping through five thousand pages didn't sound like fun, either. But I felt like I at least had to consult it. If only to get that Rebecca from Texas monkey off my back.

It took me hours to find the right spot. I read about past and present problems. The book was kind of amazing. It went all the way back to Cain and Abel — and used them as an example of what *not* to do.

Let's see. There was the standard search for buried treasure scheme where you got enemies together by making them share wealth beyond their wildest dreams. Nah, that didn't sound healthy.

Then there was one about making enemies stay by themselves on a deserted island for a month. That was interesting, but what would we tell their mothers? Besides, there's a warning that cannibalism is possible if the people still can't work out their problems. Ewww!

Hmmm. I liked the one about taking a cooking class together. They could bond over the best quiche and pizza. But I wouldn't be around long enough to benefit, so nah, I'll pass.

Then I found it! The perfect one. I could have people who don't get along bond over a common enemy. It was very fourteenth century, but I thought it would still suffice. It used many of the same principles that were used during the French Revolution, where all of the peasants — most of whom hated one another — rose together to overthrow the ultraspoiled, corrupt king and queen. Aha! I loved it. But wait, there was a warning that said this one could get mean. "You don't want thine enemy to suffer at the hands of merciless foes." Okay, there's a lot of babble here, but basically, it says you don't want your enemies to wind up liking one another only because they hate someone else. But what if that someone else is in on it? Then it's not mean!

Oh! I know the perfect person for the job!

Chapter 28
"Hooray!"
by Marina

I am so excited — Justin just called me. He is my knight in shining surf attire. I am so into him, it hurts. I was dying to share my feelings with Molly. But that was impossible — too much had happened, and we were definitely over.

But I don't want to get all down in the dump trucks! Something great just happened to me! Justin wants to meet me and Keri at the park before our very last art class. He said we'd hang out and talk. Talk! I can't believe he wants to hang out and talk to me! Yippee!

I was so excited while I got ready. I put on my best clothes, did my hair, and tore out the door. The only thing that was missing was Molly.

Chapter 29
"What a Wet and Wild Day!"
by Molly

My cousin, I swear. He's up to something —
but he's always got a trick or two handy, so
I didn't think much about this one. You have to
understand that I've been dealing with him
since birth. I mean, when we were five, our parents hid plastic Easter eggs all over our yard
for a big hunt. Well, Justin snuck out at five in
the morning, cracked them all open, and took
the candy. As a joke, he replaced the sweets
with plastic ants and street rocks. You can
imagine the mayhem he caused — and the
grounding he got. He didn't care — as long as
everyone got a laugh, Justin would do it.

So anyway, it's impossible for him to surprise
me.

This morning I was just annoyed because I
was headed to the mall. I needed some shop-

ping therapy — my life has changed a lot lately! As consolation, I was getting a new skirt. So I was going there with Kristy, then we were going to our last art class.

Oh, but no! Justin said I *had* to come to the park.

"No, I'm going to shop," I said.

"Listen to me," he pleaded. "If you don't come, I'll tell your mom that you've been sneaking into R-rated movies since you were six."

"Why should she believe you?"

"Okay, I'll also tell your dad that you stole his camera last week, then lost it at the beach."

"Don't you dare!"

"Well, then meet me at the park — and bring Kristy."

I agreed. I didn't want to argue with him anymore. I called Kristy, and we walked to the park right by our art class. We were more than steamed when we got there. Marina and Keri were there. Whatever was going on, I didn't like it. Keri walked over to Kristy and said very rudely, "What are *you* doing here?"

If Justin was trying to start World War Three, this was definitely the way to do it.

Then — *SQUISH!* I got hit in the back of the head with a water balloon. I looked up, and Justin was standing next to a bucket filled with them. "You moron!" I yelled.

126

SPLASH!

"You dumpy little brat!" I heard Keri yell. She was all wet.

One right after another — me, Keri, Marina, and Kristy — all got thwacked with two or three water balloons each. We didn't even think — we all went after Justin, hunting him down like the heathen he was. We ran in the direction the torpedoes were coming from. He was gone, but a bucket full of unused water balloons was there. We threw them as hard as we could in his direction.

Of course, I am no Olympian — neither is Marina. So I don't think we hit him once. Instead, I tried to throw one straight, and it landed smack-dab on a fire hydrant in the other direction. Meanwhile, Justin clobbered me straight in the tummy. And Marina got a good one in the tummy. Marina and I couldn't help but laugh. Then, along with Keri and Kristy — who were having a lot more luck whacking him with water bombs — we all chased him down. We threw and threw until there were no more balloons left.

We were yelling and screaming and sweating like swine. Our nice clothes were all wet and each of our heads — and hair — looked as if we'd been attacked by tornadoes. We fell down on the ground exhausted. We all looked up at one another in this totally ridiculous situation. We burst out laughing harder than I've ever laughed in my whole life. Then we laughed and laughed some more. Then we hugged and cried and jumped up and down.

I hugged Marina. Kristy hugged Keri.

I felt so good.

I felt like the hurt and fighting were over.

Chapter 30

"Whew!"

by Genny the Genie

Score!

I saw the whole zany, wild, crazy thing. I watched with delight from a low branch on a tree. Molly and Marina were so into it, they didn't even see me. Of course, since I'm invisible, no one else saw me, either. But I was there — beaming with pride when the foursome fell to the ground on top of one another, laughing.

What happened today was the whole reason I love being what I am, which is a really amazing, talented genie, if I do say so myself. I really hoped that Rebecca from Texas would hear about this.

But I couldn't think much more; I couldn't keep my peepers open. In fact, I was planning to take a nap right there in that tree. My body ached as bad as if I had been beaten up in battle. It takes a lot out of you to carry around — and fill up — a hundred water balloons!

Chapter 31
"I Liked That Fight."
by Marina

We walked for a few minutes without saying a word. I know I didn't need to talk right away. And it seemed like neither did she. We walked to art class in step with each other, smiling. I felt warm again — I had my best friend back. I looked behind me — Keri and Kristy looked like they were feeling the exact same way. I knew that the four of us would have a lot of fun together in the future. We were all growing up, and that meant we were ready for more meaningful friendships. We were also ready to open our circle of friends.

That was, by far, the best balloon-to-balloon combat I've ever been in!

We were early for class, so I said, "Molly?"

"Yes?"

"I don't ever want to fight again. Can we just forget everything that happened?" I asked.

130

"I would love to," she said. "And I'm sorry if I did anything to hurt you."

"Me, too."

Molly reached in her pocket and gave me back my half of our best friends necklace. We hugged.

"Oh my God! Oh my God!" she said, really freaking out and worrying me.

"What?" I was really worried. I hoped so hard that nothing was wrong.

"Um. Well, I didn't enter our art project," Molly cried.

"Oh, no! I didn't either! I actually told Genny *not* to turn it in!"

We were disappointed, and our spirits crumbled. Our hopes and dreams of the summer were crushed — all over a stupid, ridiculous fight.

I was really upset. What a waste!

Chapter 32
"It's Just Our Day."
by Molly

We were nearly in tears because our teacher was ready to announce the big winners — and we knew it wouldn't be us. I was even more worried that Genny *had* turned in the project under just my name. I wouldn't blame Marina for getting mad if that happened. And I didn't have the heart for a whole new fight! I loved us being made up.

He told us how much fun he'd had teaching us, blah, blah, blah. Then he got to the good stuff.

"The third prize goes to Kristy and Keri!" I was actually happy for them! That felt so much better than hating them. Kristy turned out to be so cool, I really couldn't wait to get to know Keri. I think for all of those years, the four of us badly misunderstood one another. I was glad we could try to be friends now — who knows what kind of awesome people I would have missed knowing?

The second-place winners were announced next. To our biggest surprise ever imaginable, it was us! When our teacher dude said, "Molly and Marina," we went into shock. We looked at each other and said, "Genny!"

Next came first place. I couldn't believe that I didn't even feel jealous or one tiny bit upset that the winning prize wouldn't be ours. I definitely felt like I had already won.

"It goes to Justin Gaines!"

Well, I spoke too soon. I *was* a bit jealous — but only because he'd get to man the Lobster Fest booth. I knew he'd rub it in, too.

"How did he do that?" I asked Marina.

"Just look."

What I saw was out-of-this-state, it was so awesome. He had carved a gorgeous scene of a lighthouse out of wood. Really, it was wonderful.

"Wonder where he got that lighthouse idea," Marina commented, nudging me and beaming at him.

Chapter 33
"Take That, Rebecca from Texas!"
by Genny the Genie

News of my brilliance swept through genie-mail. Not only did I have two masters who were fighting, I single-handedly got them back together. That definitely helped me look better among my worldwide peers. Even the head of the genie council put on a message board, "Genny has — once again — completed an assignment and done an excellent job. I give her an A-minus!" (A-minuses are amazing, by the way. I always get them. I would love to get an A-plus. I will do it one day!)

It's not like me to be vindictive, but I had to be. I wrote a genie-mail to Rebecca herself. It said:

so there . . .
g

I couldn't help it — I had to do it.

My own problems were definitely looking a little less, well, problematic. And that was good because my time was up. See, when my job is done, I have to go — even if twenty-eight days hadn't gone by yet. Dumb rule, but I have to follow it. I had to say *sayonara* to Molly and Marina. I knew they'd miss me — and I, of course, would miss them, too. I always hated good-byes, so to be honest, I usually avoid them. They're just too sad!

So I stopped by the beach clubhouse and was happy to see the inflatable furniture was back. Marina and Molly were catching up on everything they'd missed in the past few weeks. They thanked me for the balloon fight.

"How did you know I had anything to do with it?" I wondered.

"Because Justin told us some girl named Genny gave him the idea."

That was funny — yes, he was a good guy. I heard Molly say that he wanted the two girls to help him in the Lobster Fest booth. Molly alluded to the fact that he asked for Marina specifically. Too bad I wasn't staying — I could've made sure a little romance started brewing.

But away I went, leaving in the middle of the night as I always preferred to do.

Chapter 34
"All Better!"
by Molly and Marina

We are *we* once again. We are so glad to have each other back! We stayed up all night at the beach clubhouse talking things over. We knew that Justin had been responsible for blowing things a little out of proportion. But since he asked for Marina to help him at the lobster festival, she was super-duper happy. We both were!

We discussed Kristy and Keri. We decided it was probably a mistake not to have befriended them earlier. Then we decided that everything happens for a reason. We finally realized that having other friends can actually bring us closer. We do need to take friendship breaks!

We hugged a lot. We were happy.

There was one other thing on our agenda before we just forgot about the whole last month all together. We really wanted to know why Justin was such a pain in the booty. We called him and demanded that he come over right away.

"You really caused us a lot of grief," Molly said.

"Why did you practically mastermind a Molly versus Marina fight?" we asked. He didn't answer. We told him he better or we were telling his mother that we've seen him riding his bike without a helmet all summer.

"Okay, okay," he said, brushing back his surfer hair with his left hand. "Every time I come over here, you two are always trying to get rid of me. And every time I hang out with Kristy and Keri, they do the exact same thing. I was really just trying to get everyone together. I guess I messed up, though, because you all broke up. You do have to admit that the balloon plot was brilliant."

"Did you say you met someone named Genny?" we said.

We also brought him there because we wanted to introduce him to her. We looked all around and called her name. We were sad because she was gone.

We did find a good-bye note from her. It said,

Dear Molly and Marina,
Thanks for putting me up and feeding me pizza. I really loved hanging out with you. I know you two will be just fine.

Always remember how important and pre-cious your friendship is.

And please don't forget me — I'll never forget you.

Love,

Genny

P.S. Tell Justin good-bye for me!

Next to the note was another costume just like the one we won second prize with. Now we had one for each of us. Genny was supersweet. We put on the outfits and dedicated our best Madonna dance to her.

Chapter 35
"And So the Story Goes..."
by Genny the Genie

I begged and pleaded with Throttle to give me one more night on the beach. He threw us out into the ocean, where we rode the waves all night long. Everything was peaceful — I loved the feeling that I had done things right.

Before I went to bed, I wanted to tell Justin thanks for helping me. I wrote him a quick e-mail:

to: beachboy13
from: genny1000
hi j,
you really helped me out. thanks for orchestrating the perfect balloon fight. i was impressed. if you ever want a new career, i think i know one that might be good for you.
talk to you soon,
genny

Immediately, I heard that cute little "Bling!" and I got a message back. I was excited to carry on a cyber conversation with my good buddy Justin. I opened it up and was so surprised that it wasn't from him.

It was from Rebecca from Texas. Yuck!

All it said was, *"i'll see ya soon!"*